BV

"That wasn't what I meant at all!"

Rosie stopped and stamped her foot in anger. "You know it wasn't."

Fergus said bluntly, "Well, of course, I know. I cannot imagine why you should have any interest in me as a person. We scarcely know each other, now do we?"

She looked up into his quiet face. "No—no we don't."

"That can, of course, be remedied. Indeed, I thought that we were verging on a kind of cautious friendship."

Rosie smiled suddenly. "Yes—well—" she put out a hand "—all right, Fergus."

His hand was firm and very large, and for some reason, she wanted to leave her own hand in its grasp. She withdrew it prudently, and Fergus bent and kissed her gently.

Betty Neels is well-known for her romances set in the Netherlands, which is hardly surprising. She married a Dutchman and spent the first twelve years of their marriage living in Holland and working as a nurse. Today, she and her husband make their home in an ancient stone cottage in England's West Country, but they return to Holland often. She loves to explore tiny villages and tour privately owned homes there, in order to lend an air of authenticity to the background of her books.

Books by Betty Neels

HARLEQUIN ROMANCE

3105—THE GIRL WITH GREEN EYES
3131—A SUITABLE MATCH
3149—ROSES HAVE THORNS
3161—A LITTLE MOONLIGHT
3185—THE MOST MARVELLOUS SUMMER
3197—THE FINAL TOUCH

Don't miss any of our special offers. Write to us at the following address for information on our newest releases.

Harlequin Reader Service
P.O. Box 1397, Buffalo, NY 14240
Canadian address: P.O. Box 603,
Fort Erie, Ont. L2A 5X3

A KIND OF MAGIC
Betty Neels

Harlequin Books

TORONTO • NEW YORK • LONDON
AMSTERDAM • PARIS • SYDNEY • HAMBURG
STOCKHOLM • ATHENS • TOKYO • MILAN
MADRID • WARSAW • BUDAPEST • AUCKLAND

Original hardcover edition published in 1991
by Mills & Boon Limited

ISBN 0-373-03208-0

Harlequin Romance first edition July 1992

A KIND OF MAGIC

CHAPTER ONE

THE bright sunshine of early May, pouring through the latticed windows of the old house, shone on to the short dark curls of the girl bent over the case she was packing with a kind of controlled ferocity.

She was young, built on Junoesque lines, and tall with a lovely face and dark eyes heavily fringed with black lashes. The face was marred at the moment by her heavy frown.

'I cannot think what Granny is about,' she observed to the middle-aged lady—an older, gently faded version of herself sitting and watching her. 'Mother, she is eighty years old; why on earth does she want to go trekking across the Highlands of Scotland...?'

'Not trekking, Rosie—she won't have to move from the train if she doesn't wish to!' Mrs Macdonald heaved a sentimental sigh. 'I think it is rather touching that she should want to see the surroundings of her childhood.'

'Well, she won't see much from the train.' Rosie then added because of her mother's unhappy look, 'Well, if it makes her happy. But why me? There's Aunt Carrie...'

'Your granny and Aunt Carrie don't get on, dear. It is only for a week, and I dare say there will be some interesting people on the train.' She paused. 'Aren't you going to take the cream jersey? You look so nice in it, and it doesn't take up any room...'

'Anyway, you never know,' continued her mother vaguely, and Rosie, guessing her parent's thoughts, said baldly,

'There will be Americans on the train, Mother, and possibly a German or two, all married and over fifty.'

'Oh, I do hope not,' said Mrs Macdonald. She had never quite understood why Rosie, at twenty-five, was still unmarried. She was as pretty as a picture, had any number of friends and, to her mother's knowledge, had turned down—in the nicest possible manner—several offers of marriage.

'Don't you want to get married?' she voiced her thoughts out loud.

'Oh, yes, Mother, dear. But I haven't met him yet...'

'There was that nice Percy Walls,' said Mrs Macdonald.

'Pooh!' replied Rosie strongly. 'He only talked about food and how clever he was. If I had married him I would have been a doormat, everlastingly cooking snacks.'

'He did like his food,' conceded Mrs Macdonald, 'but he was keen on you, darling.'

'Just because I can cook.' Rosie rolled up a pleated skirt in a ruthless fashion, and stuffed it into her case. 'Very surely being keen isn't enough, Mother. The man I marry must dote on me, cherish and love me for always, even when I'm bad-tempered or sneezing my head off.' She closed the case, and added briskly, 'I don't imagine there is such a man...'

'He sounds worth waiting for,' said Mrs Macdonald. 'I must admit that a man's love can be tried to the utmost when one has a heavy cold. Though I must say that your father is an exception.' She sounded a little smug, and Rosie laughed and dropped a kiss on her mother's cheek as she went to the dressing-table. 'Mother, Father is the nicest man I know... How much money shall I need to take, do you think?'

'Your granny said not to take any, but I think you had better take some; she forgets sometimes. Are you not looking forward to this trip at all, love?'

'Well, it will be nice to be in Scotland again, only a week isn't long enough—I'd love to stay up in the Highlands for a long time, walk perhaps, or drive around. But I've only got two weeks' holiday, and Miss Porter wants to go away in June, so I'll have to be there to do some of her work.'

Rosie had spoken cheerfully; she disliked her job as a shorthand typist at Messrs Crabbe, Crabbe and Twitchett, the leading solicitors in the small country town in Wiltshire where she lived, but she had never said so; her father had lost almost all of his capital some years previously when the shares he held became almost worthless, and in order to keep his home in Scotland intact he had handed it over to a cousin and taken the job of agent on a large estate in Wiltshire. Neither he nor her mother had ever complained, although Rosie knew that they missed their home as much as she did. She had set about learning shorthand and typing, got herself a job, and consoled herself with the thought that their home in Scotland was, at least, still in the family.

Her grandmother lived in Edinburgh with her un-married daughter who was older than Rosie's father—a wispy lady who was seldom able to complete a sen-tence, and was possessed of a meekness which irritated the old lady, a forceful person who browbeat her despite the care Aunt Carrie took of her. Rosie was able to see her very seldom; the journey to Scotland was expensive and long, and she suspected that her parents were reluctant to visit their old home now that her father's cousin lived there. Now she had been bidden to accompany the old lady on a train tour of the Highlands. 'To revive old memories,' her grandmother had said, and had explained her plan more fully by letter.

'I hear that the train is splendidly equipped and very well staffed. I shall not need to exert myself, but of course I need a companion. You will come with me, Rosie.'

'Of course you must go,' her father had observed. 'It will be a pleasant holiday for you; besides, it will give Carrie a week of peace and quiet.' He hadn't seen his sister for some time but he had vivid memories of his mother keeping her under her thumb. A week of freedom would do her good. So all the arrangements had been made; Rosie was to travel up to Edinburgh by train, spend the night at her grandmother's house, and escort her to the station on the following day. There wouldn't be many passengers, she had been told, and she had been sent the brochure so that she would have some idea what to expect. It had looked rather fun, and they would see many of the places she had known so well as a child, only she thought it unlikely that she would have much chance to poke around on her own. Granny had made it quite clear that she expected constant attention and companionship.

She and her mother went downstairs presently into the kitchen, and began to get supper while they argued amicably as to whether Rosie's jersey suit would be better than her lovat corduroy skirt and country shirt with her matching gilet over.

'It could be quite chilly still,' argued Mrs Macdonald. 'On the other hand the jersey is useful. I wish you could have had some new clothes...'

'No need—I've got several thin tops with me, and I'll take the skirt and gilet. There's the shirtwaister if it gets really warm.'

Her father came in presently, and she went to lay the table in the small dining-room, seldom used, but this evening seemed a special occasion.

Her father drove her to the station the next morning in the rather battered Land Rover. He hadn't much to say; he was a quiet man, tall and thin and hardworking; he looked after the estate with the same care with which he had run his own family home in Scotland. Rosie wished with all her heart that he and her mother could have been coming with her; more than that she wished that they could go back to her home there. She sat up straighter; it did no good to repine. It would be nice to see Granny again even though she was a tartar; she listened carefully to her father's last-minute messages, kissed him goodbye, and got into the train.

'I'll be back in a week,' she told him. 'I'll phone and let you know which train I'll be on.'

Her grandmother had sent enough money for her fare and for a taxi to get her to King's Cross Station, and she joined the long queue. She was seldom in London, she didn't like it much, and she was glad when she finally reached the station with time to spare for coffee before she needed to get on to the train. It was more than six years since she had been at King's Cross; that was when they had left Scotland, and Rosie remembered how unhappy she had been. Her spirits lifted at the thought of going back, even if only for a week, and she

got on to the train, found a corner seat, and prepared
to while away the journey with a paperback until the
train had left London and its suburbs, and begun its
race to the north.

Waverley Station hadn't changed; it was in the heart
of Edinburgh, and she gave an unconscious sigh of
pleasure as she went in search of a taxi. Her grandmother lived on the other side of Princes Street, in a
grey granite house, tall and narrow, one of a terrace of
such houses in a narrow, winding street near Queen Street
Gardens, surprisingly quiet although there was the
constant hum of traffic from Princes Street and Queen
Street. She got out of the taxi, and stood for a moment
on the pavement looking up at her grandmother's house.
It hadn't changed at all; there was the same solid door,
the same dark green curtains at the narrow windows.
She mounted the steps to the door and banged the
knocker, and after a few moments it was partly opened
by Elspeth, the elderly maid who had been with her
grandmother ever since Rosie could remember.

She must be all of seventy, thought Rosie, embracing
her warmly, but she seemed ageless, her iron-grey hair
scraped back into a stiff bun, her bony frame erect in
its black dress.

Elspeth led the way into the narrow hall, and opened
a door. 'Yer granny's waiting. I'll leave ye a wee while
before I bring in the tea.'

She gave Rosie a little push and shut the door on her.
Old Mrs Macdonald was sitting bolt upright in a high-
backed chair. She was an imposing figure, tall and stout
with dark hair only lightly streaked with silver. She was
handsome, with dark eyes and a straight nose above an

obstinate mouth. She hadn't changed, thought Rosie, crossing the room to kiss her.

'You had a good journey?' asked her grandmother, the question uttered in a voice which expected no reply. 'Your mother and father are well?'

'Very well, Granny. They sent their love.'

'Sit down, child, and let me look at you. Still not wed? There is, perhaps, a young man?'

'No—not one I wish to marry. Where is Aunt Carrie, Granny?'

'She got it into her head to make a cake for your arrival. She will be in the kitchen.'

The door opened as she spoke, and Aunt Carrie came in. Rosie remembered her as a pretty, rather faded woman who adored her brother and sister-in-law. She was still pretty, but she looked dispirited and worn out. She probably was, reflected Rosie as she went to greet her, living with Granny day in and day out. She would have a week to herself now, and not before time.

Aunt Carrie kissed her fondly. 'I made a cake, it seemed... You look well, dear, and not a day... You're not...?'

'No,—Aunt Carrie. I'm waiting for a millionaire, handsome and generous, who will lavish the world's goods upon me.'

Mrs Macdonald gave a ladylike snort. 'That is a worldly attitude to be deplored, Rosie.'

Rosie winked at Aunt Carrie and said, suitably meek, 'Yes, Granny.'

They had tea presently, and Rosie lavished praise upon the cake while she listened to her grandmother's plans for the train journey, which would start in the morning. Her plans concerned herself and her comfort, for she

was a selfish old lady. Rosie, listening to them, wondered if they clashed with their journey; she had read
the brochure with its carefully planned itinerary, and it
allowed little room for independent plans for the passengers, and as far as she could see the whole journey
was so meticulously arranged that only the most discontented and selfish person could take exception to it.
Of course, her grandmother was both discontented *and*
selfish.

'This is, of course, a great treat for you, Rosie,' observed her grandparent complacently.

Rosie replied suitably, wondering silently just how
much of a treat it would be.

She managed to have a word with her aunt the next
morning. 'Do have a good time, Aunt Carrie,' she urged.
'You've a whole week, think of all the things you can
do. You must have friends?'

'Well, your grandmother doesn't care for visitors, dear,
but I meet them from time to time while I'm shopping.'

She had gone a pretty pink, and Rosie said, 'Is he
nice, Aunt Carrie?'

The pink deepened. 'A retired solicitor, dear, but of
course I have your granny to look after.'

'Stuff!' retorted Rosie fiercely. 'There is Elspeth, and
Granny can afford a companion. Does she know?'

'No. And there's not much point... I mean, we're
just friends.'

'Well, make the most of him.' They stood listening to
her grandmother's voice giving brisk orders. 'It's time
we went—we have to be on the platform before nine
o'clock.'

They were met at the station by two pleasant young
men, who whisked away their luggage and took them to

one of the lounges to wait for the train. The room was full, and a score of faces turned to them as they were introduced, before Mrs Macdonald was seated with suitable care in a chair, and offered coffee. Rosie sat down not too near her, and over coffee exchanged names with those around her. Americans mostly, a sprinkling of Germans, and a haughty-looking woman with a meek husband who had flown up from London. All very VIP, thought Rosie, making suitable replies to friendly questions. She had been right; there was no one there under fifty. They were all prosperous-looking couples, well dressed and pleased with themselves. Within five minutes they had asked her name, and from then on she was 'Rosie', despite the look of affront upon her grandmother's face.

They boarded the train in style, with a piper to lead them, and once there, sitting convivially in the observation car, they were offered champagne. Rosie, careful not to look at Mrs Macdonald, enjoyed hers. Later, after the train had got under way, Rosie led her grandmother to their cabins. The old lady had taken a long time deciding whether Rosie should share a cabin with her or whether they should be apart. Rosie was glad now that she had made up her mind to be on her own; doubtless it would mean that she would have to nip to and fro a good deal, but it would be worth it. She sat her grandmother down in the beautifully appointed cabin, and unpacked for her, and rang the bell for the stewardess so that orders might be given concerning morning tea, a tin of biscuits in case of hunger during the night and a warm drink before retiring. The stewardess had a soft Highland voice and a gentle face. Everything would be done just as Mrs Macdonald wished, she promised.

'You can unpack later,' said Mrs Macdonald. 'I will go back to the observation car, but you must go with me—I find the corridors difficult. I must see someone about our table...'

'I heard someone say that we sit where we like,' remarked Rosie. 'Rather nice, for we can get to know everyone.'

Her grandmother gave her a steely look. 'I shall ask for a table for two to be reserved for us. And now come along, Rosie, we have wasted enough time sitting here idly.'

Rosie, who hadn't sat down once, said nothing, merely led the way back to the observation car where a good many of the passengers had forgathered. She sat the old lady down in a small armchair so placed that if she didn't wish to talk to anyone there would be no need, accepted the sherry they were offered, and sat down to drink it. It was good sherry but she didn't waste time drinking it. With a muttered excuse she skipped away back to her cabin, where she unpacked and tidied everything away, did her face and hair and, armed with the itinerary, went back, just in time to join her grandmother for lunch.

The old lady had had her way, of course; they were to sit at a table for two for the entire journey. Rosie, listening to her grandmother's annoyed remarks concerning the lack of companionship which it was evident she would be called upon to endure, wished she could have joined in the cheerful talk at the larger tables. She spoke soothingly, promised constant attendance in the future and, being a sensible girl, enjoyed the excellent meal while making suitable conversation.

'I shall rest,' declared Mrs Macdonald as they finished their coffee. 'There is a visit this afternoon, I believe. We stop at Spean Bridge in order to drive there, but I shall not go—I know the house and I should have enjoyed meeting old friends again, but I have to think of my health. You will stay with me, Rosie—I like to be read to while I rest.'

Rosie swallowed disappointment, and said, 'Yes, Granny,' in a voice carefully devoid of expression. The train had turned north at Craigendoran Junction, the country was dramatically beautiful, with mountains still snow-capped ringing the horizon, and soon they would be crossing Rannoch Moor. Years ago she had walked part of its lonely road with her father, and she wanted to see it all again.

'You don't wish to see the moor? We are almost at Bridge of Orchy——' She glanced out of the window. 'There are several people on the walkway...'

'My health is more important than sentimental re-membrances at the moment. Tomorrow I shall have re-covered sufficiently to look around me.'

So they made their way back to Mrs Macdonald's cabin, where Rosie finally settled her on her bed and obediently opened the book she was to read. It was a dull book, full of long words, and she read badly be-cause she was listening to the cheerful departure of everyone else. She ventured a peep out of the window, and saw them climbing aboard the special coach which was to carry them to the various places to be visited. There was a lot of laughing and chatter, and she longed to be there too. She reminded herself sternly that she had come to look after Granny, and went back to the book.

Ten minutes after the coach had left Mrs Macdonald went to sleep, and presently Rosie closed the book, opened the cabin door quietly, and went to stand in the corridor to take stock of her surroundings. The train would leave for Fort William soon, and wait there for the coach, and after making sure that her grandmother was sleeping soundly she went to the observation car and through its doors to the platform beyond. It was a fresh day, threatening rain, and she stayed there until the train started on its way to Fort William where it would pick up its passengers. But before that she was summoned back to her grandmother's cabin, to find that lady wishing to be tidied after her nap and to take tea.

They had just finished when the rest of the party got on to the train again, full of their pleasant afternoon. They gathered round Mrs Macdonald and Rosie, not noting the former's icy lack of interest, but Rosie listened happily, glad to talk to them, and rather taken aback when a cheerful matron from Chicago remarked that it was a shame that her granny was sick, and wouldn't they like to sit with them at dinner?

Rosie listened to her grandmother explaining in well-modulated tones that conversation gave her a headache, and it was essential that she should take her meals without distraction. The Americans were nice; they offered sympathy with a friendliness which Rosie would have liked to have reciprocated.

So they dined presently, she and her grandmother, sitting in a near silence, Mrs Macdonald in black crêpe and pearls, and Rosie in silk jersey, the old lady apparently oblivious of the convivial atmosphere around them. Rosie was quite glad when the old lady said that she would go to bed shortly after dinner. Of course, an hour passed before she was in her bed, and another half-hour before Rosie was told that she might go to her own cabin.

'A pleasant day,' commented Mrs Macdonald.' I hope you'll make sure that I am called with China tea at half-past seven, Rosie?'

Rosie simply said, 'Yes, Granny' to both remarks, and sped back to the observation car to spend the next hour or so exchanging light-hearted views and opinions with everyone there.

The next day the train took them to Mallaig, and although Mrs Macdonald refused to get out of the train Rosie was dispatched into the village to get postcards and stamps—an excuse to walk briskly down to the harbour and watch the ferry from Skye come in, where she was swept into a friendly group of passengers. The pleasant little interlude cheered her before going back to her grandmother, to sit with her, watching the familiar countryside and listening to the old lady's reminiscences. They were going back over Rannoch Moor again to stay for the night at Bridge of Orchy, and the scene was familiar. Rosie's old home wasn't far away— a nice old house tucked away at the foot of the mountains behind Oban. She longed to see it again, but her grandmother, who had never approved of her father allowing it to pass into the hands of his cousin, had stated categorically that she had no wish to see it. It was a pointless remark, for the train didn't go within a dozen miles of it.

There was another visit to a local country estate that evening, but Mrs Macdonald declared herself too tired to go. She and Rosie dined alone to the great inconvenience of the train staff, Rosie thought, although they presented smiling faces when her grandmother requested dinner to be served at the usual time. Everyone else had gone off in the coach and would have a buffet supper at the house they were to visit.

Rosie settled her grandparent for the night, went back to the observation car, and was presently overwhelmed by the returning passengers, eager to tell her about the house they had seen, and the buffet super. They were kind, and concerned that she was having such a dull time of it.

'But tomorrow we're all going to the wildlife park,' one woman remarked. 'Your grandmother could come in the coach and be put down at the hotel in Aviemore, Rosie. That would be nice and quiet for her, and you could come with us . . .'

It sounded a splendid idea, Rosie agreed. 'But I'll have to see how Granny feels about it,' she reminded them.

She had been too hopeful. In the morning Mrs Macdonald declared that she intended to visit the hotel by the station where she had stayed years ago. 'With your grandfather, dear—a sentimental visit I have long looked forward to.' When Rosie said hopefully that she might like to be on her own there, she was told at once that probably the emotion stirred up by fond memories might upset her grandmother; it was essential that she had Rosie beside her.

Rosie watched the coach drive away once more and, presently warned by Jamie, the guide, as he got into the coach, that the train would leave in an hour's time for Perth and Stirling, the pair of them walked the very short distance from the train to the hotel.

It had of course, changed hands. Which didn't stop her grandmother insisting upon seeing round the hotel, pausing from time to time to make some blistering remark about the changes in the rooms. The owner was patient and courteous, but even his politeness wore thin when Mrs Macdonald criticised the colour scheme in the dining-room in no uncertain terms.

Time I did something, decided Rosie, and asked if they might have coffee.

They drank it in the pleasant lounge on the other side of the foyer and after a short time she said, 'We should be going back, Granny, the train's due to leave in ten minutes...'

'I cannot be hurried, my dear. I intend to take a quick look at the gardens at the back of the hotel—five minutes only I promise you—and I wish to be alone. Wait here.'

Rosie paid the bill, and went to the hotel entrance. She could see the train clearly enough, five minutes would suffice to get her grandmother back on board. She knew that the schedule was strict, for the train had to fit in exactly with the normal timetable, and they had been warned in the nicest possible way by Jamie that if anyone missed it they would have to find their way to the next stopping-place. She glanced at her watch—her grandmother had been gone for five minutes and there was no sign of her.

The gardens behind the hotel were neatly laid out with a variety of shrubs and beds of flowers, petering out into rough grass hedged with gorse and broom, ferns and, later in the year, heather. She found her grandmother there huddled on the ground, one leg bent awkwardly. Mrs Macdonald's face was paper-white, but she had lost very little of her brisk manner.

'My leg,' she explained 'I tripped. The ankle...'

'I'll get help,' said Rosie, who when necessary could be just as brisk as her granny, and sped back to the hotel, where she sent the owner and one of the waiters to carry her grandmother in, and then turned and ran back to the station.

Will, one of the stewards, was on the platform.

'We're off in just under five minutes, Miss Macdonald,' he began.

Rosie told him what had happened, and before she had finished the train manager had joined them.

'We shall have to stay behind,' she told him. 'We'll never be able to get my grandmother on to the train, and she needs a doctor quickly. I know that you have to leave on the dot. Could someone pack our things and send them back here on one of the local trains? I can't think of anything else to do...'

'I'll come to the hotel.' The manager glanced at his watch, and began marching her back. 'I'm so very sorry, but you do see that the journey can't be delayed or altered...?'

'Yes, of course. We shall be quite all right here, but I think that if it's a sprain or a break we shall have to stay for a while until something can be arranged.'

They had reached the hotel, and found Mrs Macdonald laid out on a big sofa. She had lost her shoe when she fell, and the ankle was badly swollen. She opened her eyes as they reached her, and said peevishly, 'I intend to remain here until a doctor has examined me. Rosie will make the necessary arrangements. Good of you to come.'

The manager was a nice youngish man; he said all that was proper and, with his eye on the time, wished her a speedy recovery, and promised that she would hear from him.

'I'll phone you from Stirling,' he promised, 'and I'll see about your luggage. Has someone phoned for a doctor? There should be one at Crianlarich and several in Oban.'

'Don't worry, the hotel owner will know.' Rosie added urgently, 'Don't, for heaven's sake, miss the train.'

'I hate to leave you both——' he shook her hand '—but there's nothing else for it.'

The train gave an impatient toot, and he turned and ran.

There were several people fussing around her grandmother, not quite sure what to do first.

'Scissors, please,' said Rosie, 'a bowl of cold water and a napkin. How long will it take the doctor to get here?'

She took her grandmother's hand and gave it a heartening squeeze. 'I'm so sorry, Granny, we'll have you comfortable in a little while.' She was carefully cutting the black stocking, and easing it off the swollen foot.

'I don't know much about it, but I don't think it's broken. I'm going to lay a cold cloth over it. There…and if someone will help me we'll put some cushions behind you; you'll feel easier sitting up a little.'

One of the waitresses came in with a cup of tea, and the hotel owner came back to say that most fortunately Dr Finlay at Crianlarich had just returned from early-morning fishing, and was driving over. They were to make the patient comfortable, but were not to move her.

Rosie studied her grandmother's pale face anxiously. 'How far away is Crianlarich?' she asked,

'Twelve miles, but it's a good road. He'll be a wee while yet; ye'd best have a cup of tea while waiting.'

She drank her tea gratefully, applied more cold cloths, and made quiet, heartening small talk—to be interrupted suddenly by Mrs Macdonald.

'We are so near home...'

'Would you like me to telephone Uncle Donald, Granny? Perhaps we could...?'

'Certainly not. When your father saw fit to let Donald have his family home I washed my hands of the whole affair.'

Rosie murmured a nothing. She knew that her grandmother had blamed her father for leaving Scotland, and that he had never told her how he had come to lose most of his capital and been forced to make the heart-rending decision to hand over the house to his prosperous cousin. Privately Rosie had never understood why her uncle couldn't have lent her father the money to come about, but he was a hard man, made harder by the wealth he had acquired by marrying an heiress. She had never liked him anyway; years ago when she had been on a visit to his house she had come upon him beating one of his dogs. She had caught his arm and hung on to it and kicked his shins, calling him a brute, and then screaming at the top of her voice until several people came running to see what was the matter. He had never forgiven her for that.

Her grandmother was looking alarmingly pale. Rosie renewed the cold compress, persuaded her grandmother to take a sip of brandy, and prayed silently that the doctor would come soon.

Her prayers were answered; the slight commotion in the hotel entrance heralded the doctor's arrival.

He came in unhurriedly, an immensely tall, broad-shouldered man, dark-haired and dark-eyed with a long straight nose and a firm mouth. He wasted no time.

'Doctor Cameron,' he stated. 'Doctor Finlay was called to a birth, and he asked me to take over. What is the trouble?'

He gave Rosie a nod and a quick questioning glance; she could have been yesterday's newspaper, she reflected with a touch of peevishness.

'My grandmother fell. Her ankle is swollen and very painful...'

He took Mrs Macdonald's hand. 'A nasty shock for you, Mrs...?'

'Macdonald,' said Rosie. 'My grandmother is eighty years old.'

He gave her a look which put her in her place. 'Let's look at it.'

He was very gentle, keeping up a steady flow of quiet questions as he examined the swollen joint. 'A sprain— a nasty one, but I think nothing is broken. It will be best if you stay here in bed for a few days with your ankle bandaged, and when you are more yourself you must go to Oban and have an X-ray. You live in Scotland?'

'Edinburgh. My granddaughter and I were taking the train tour of the Highlands.' Mrs Macdonald opened her eyes and studied his face. 'And where are you from, may I ask?'

He didn't answer directly. 'I'm staying with Doctor Finlay for some fishing.' He smiled at her suddenly and with great charm. 'Now I want you to rest quietly while that ankle settles down. I shall write you up for some-thing to relieve the pain, and within a couple of days or so you should be well enough to go for an X-ray. If it is, as I think, a sprain, then there is no reason why you shouldn't go home and rest there. Now I am going to strap it firmly, and later, when you may get up, a viscopaste stocking must be applied.'

Mrs Macdonald might be a crotchety, selfish old lady but she had courage; she uttered no sound as he attended to the ankle, and when Rosie said urgently, 'Oh, Granny's fainted!' the doctor said calmly, 'Good, pass me that crêpe bandage and let us get finished before she comes round.' He gave her a quick look. 'You have arranged to stay here?'

'Not yet.' She spoke sharply, 'I've had no time.'

'Well, see about it now, will you? Get a room, and I'll carry Mrs Macdonald up, then you get her undressed and in bed, and I'll take another look at her before I go.'

There were two rooms on the first floor, she was told, with a communicating door and, providing she was prepared to pay for it, fortunately room service was available.

'Good, we'll have them. Could someone get the bed ready for my grandmother? The doctor will carry her up...'

There were plenty of willing helpers; Mrs Macdonald was carried up to her room and laid on the bed, and a chambermaid stayed to help get her into bed, offering a nightie and extra pillows, and helping Rosie to arrange a chair at the foot of the bed so that the bedclothes might be draped over it.

The doctor nodded approvingly when he came to see his patient again.

'Your grandmother will do very well,' he observed. 'I can see that you're a sensible lass. From these parts?'

'Yes.' She paused. 'Well, I was born near here but we live in England now.'

He stood studying her, looking down his long nose in a manner which she found annoying. 'Married?'

'No.'

He smiled. 'A woman of refreshingly few words.' Then he added to surprise her, 'Are you all right for money?'

'Why, yes, thank you. It is kind of you to ask.'

'Nothing kind about it—common sense in the circumstances. It would have gone on the bill.'

She ignored this. 'Will you come to see my grandmother again?' She is old, it must have been a shock . . .'

'I'll be over tomorrow, in the morning.' He stared at her, and added, 'Unless you would rather Dr Finlay took over the case?'

'Why do you say that? Granny is perfectly satisfied . . .'

'Good.' He spoke carelessly. 'Perhaps by tomorrow you and I will like each other a little better. Good day to you, Miss Macdonald.'

He had gone leaving her bewildered and decidedly ill-tempered.

CHAPTER TWO

ROSIE was kept busy for the rest of the morning; she telephoned Elspeth and promised to ring again that evening, then she phoned her mother.

'Are you going to let Uncle Donald know?' she asked, 'Inverard is barely a dozen miles from the hotel; you could go there...'

'Granny won't hear of it. Oh, Mother, I'd love to see it again, only not with Uncle Donald there, and I think Granny feels the same. She never did like him...'

'Will you be all right? Is there anything we can do, Rosie?'

'Nothing, Mother, for the moment. I'll phone you tomorrow when the doctor's been again.'

She spent the rest of the day with her grandmother, leaving her only for long enough to have a meal and answer the anxious enquiries of the train manager. Their luggage had been sent back to Bridge of Orchy in the late afternoon, and was there anything that he could do to help them? He added that the crew and passengers on the train sent their best wishes for Mrs Macdonald's speedy recovery.

'We shall be doing this same trip next week,' he reminded her, 'and if you are still at the hotel we shall call on you both. Perhaps you will leave a message if you depart before then?'

She thanked him; he had been kind and more than concerned for their welfare, although it had been no fault of his or his staff. She felt even more grateful when their luggage arrived, and with it a splendid basket of fruit for her grandmother with the train staff's best wishes.

Dr Cameron had left sleeping pills for her grandmother so that the old lady slept for a good part of the night. All the same, she woke in the early morning wanting her pillows rearranged, a cup of tea, and Rosie's company.

The hotel bedrooms had tea and coffee, sugar and milk arranged by an electric kettle. Rosie made tea for them both, and sat with her grandmother until that lady dozed off once more, enabling her to return to her own room, shower and dress, and do the best she could with a tired face.

Dr Cameron came soon after breakfast. Mrs Macdonald, refreshed after a wash, a changed nightie and a light breakfast, greeted him with a tart, 'Well, young man, and what do you intend to do this morning?'

His expression remained professionally calm. 'Merely a quick look at that ankle. How did you sleep?'

He glanced at Rosie standing on the other side of the bed. 'Rather wakeful?'

'I have had considerable pain,' said Mrs Macdonald waspishly. 'Rosie gave me tea—oh, about four o'clock this morning, I suppose, and another of your pills; I dozed off eventually.'

The old lady then asked her granddaughter, 'At what time did you leave me, Rosie?'

'Ten to six, Granny.'

Dr Cameron gave her a hard stare; that would account for her pallor and her cross face. 'If I might see this ankle?' he prompted gently.

The limb was inspected, pronounced as satisfactory as circumstances allowed, and made comfortable.

'Quite satisfactory,' pronounced Dr Cameron, 'but I believe that you will benefit from a change of sleeping tablets. A good night's sleep is essential.' He forbore from looking at her heavy-eyed granddaughter as he spoke. 'I have a busy day ahead of me; perhaps it might be as well if your granddaughter were to return to the surgery with me now, collect them, and return with me—I have to go further along the road to a shepherd's croft on Rannoch Moor.'

He didn't wait for Mrs Macdonald to object to this. 'If you could come right away?' he asked Rosie. 'I have Finlay's patients to visit...'

It would be simply lovely to have a breath of air. 'You'll be all right, Granny?'

'It seems that I shall have to be. Tell someone that I shall be alone until you return; I can only hope that I shall not need your services.'

'Try and have a nap,' said Rosie, 'I shan't be long.'

She fetched a cardigan, and followed the doctor out of the hotel, to squeeze into the small, shabby car, hardly suitable for two splendidly built persons, and be driven away without more ado.

It was a bright clear morning, the country through which they drove was remote and grandly rugged, snow-capped mountains filled the horizon, late primroses carpeted the rough grass. The lonely moor was at their backs as they climbed to Tyndrum Upper and over the viaducts towards Crianlarich.

Rose sighed with the pleasure of it all, and the doctor asked,

'You know this part of the world?' He glanced at her. 'You said you were born near here?'

'Yes.'

'Would you not like to return?'

'Yes.' She looked out of the window at the grandeur all around her; not a soul in sight, and they hadn't passed a car, only slowed once or twice for a leisurely sheep with her lambs. She knew that if she got out of the car there wouldn't be a sound—only the quiet breath of the wind and the birds. She wanted above all things to stay in this magnificent solitude.

'Then why don't you? I imagine you could get a job easily enough—the hotels are always short-staffed.' He sounded uninterested, carrying on some kind of conversation out of politeness.

Rose said stonily, 'I already have a job, and I live with my parents. Why did you ask me to come with you? There was no need; you could have handed in the pills on your way back, since you have to go and see a patient on the moor.'

'You looked as though you needed a change of scene. Your disturbed night appears to have left you decidedly whey-faced and peevish.'

She said hotly, 'I don't like you, Dr Cameron.'

'I dare say not. That's only because you're such a cross-patch. I think you must be quite a nice girl in kinder circumstances.' He slowed the car as they reached the outskirts of Crianlarich—a scattering of cottages on either side of the road, and then the main street.

'Do you want to come in?' he asked as he stopped before a solid house opposite the church. 'I'll be a couple of minutes.'

'Thank you, no.' She turned an exquisite profile to him, and didn't see his smile.

She regretted her words; he was all of ten minutes.

'A small boy with a bead in his ear,' he told her, squeezing in beside her again. 'I knew you wouldn't mind, and his mother was upset.'

'You got it out?'

His firm mouth twitched. 'Yes. Take these, will you? See that your grandmother has one at bedtime; that should ensure that you both have a good night's sleep.'

He dropped the small bottle of pills into her lap and started the car. He had very little to say after that, apart from the bare minimum of conversation good manners dictated.

She got out of the car at the hotel, and then poked her head through the window. 'I'm sorry I was cross, and thank you for the ride.'

'Think nothing of it, Miss Macdonald. In these sparsely populated parts it behoves one to offer a helping hand to all and sundry, does it not?'

She wasn't sure if she liked being called 'all and sundry'. She said starchily, quite sorry that she had apologised, 'We shall expect you in the morning, Dr Cameron.'

He nodded coolly, and shot away, and she watched the car disappear along the lonely road.

She was in time to pour oil on the troubled waters of her grandmother's insistence that she should interview the chef so that she might order exactly what she wanted for her lunch.

'A light meal, Granny,' said Rosie soothingly. 'Dr Cameron told me that if you kept to a light diet for a few days it will make your recovery much quicker.'

She took the menu from the huffy chef's hand. 'There is salmon—now, poached salmon with a potato or two would be delicious, and I see there is clear soup...just right.' She caught the man's eye. 'And perhaps the chef would be so kind as to make you a junket? If I were to have the same perhaps that would be less trouble?'

The chef went away appeased, and she sat down and regaled Mrs Macdonald with an account of her brief trip. Not that there was much to say, but she took care to make it sound as though she and Dr Cameron were on the best of terms.

Presently her grandmother dozed, and Rosie went down to the hotel lounge for coffee. There weren't many people there. The guests at that time of year were for the most part walkers along the walkway between Glasgow and Fort William; they spent a night or stopped for a meal before taking to the road again. There was a party of them sitting on the hotel steps, resting their feet while they drank their coffee, and they called her to join them. They were a cheerful lot, and she envied them, going at their own pace, taking perhaps three days over the walk, stopping where they wanted to with the leisure to stand and stare as much as they wanted. The vague idea that perhaps she might manage a day to walk a few miles crossed her mind, although she had no idea how that could be arranged; it depended very much on how her grandmother progressed, and it was more than likely that as soon as she was fit enough to leave for a few hours she would want to go back to Edinburgh. She drank her coffee, wished her companions a pleasant journey, and went back to the invalid.

Mrs Macdonald was at her most pernickety. Nothing was right; she was too hot, too cold, bored, and then

peevishly wishing to be left in peace and quiet. Rosie
did her best to cope with this variety of moods; her
grandmother, despite her age, was an active person, and
to lie inactive in bed was almost worse than the pain of
her sprained ankle. Rosie read until she was hoarse,
listened to her grandmother reminiscing about the days
of her childhood and youth, and ventured to suggest,
not for the first time, that her Uncle Donald would visit
her if she cared to let him know of her accident.

'Certainly not,' declared the old lady indignantly. 'I'm
surprised that you should suggest such a thing.' She
sounded wistful. 'Your Uncle Donald never writes. I am,
after all, his aunt, but he has cut himself off from his
family.'

'Did you quarrel?'

'That is my business, Rosie.'

As she got ready for bed that night Rosie made up her
mind to speak to Dr Cameron in the morning. Surely
her grandmother was well enough to be taken back to
Edinburgh? Elspeth and Aunt Carrie would be there and,
if necessary, a nurse. She had phoned her mother that
evening, making light of everything, assuring her that
she would be home just as soon as possible. In any case,
she reflected, she would have to go home at the end of
two weeks; she would be needed at the office, and one
week had gone already. She slept badly, and woke to a
morning dark with tumultuous clouds racing across the
sky, bringing a fine rain on a strengthening wind.

Dr Cameron came during the morning, examining the
ankle, which was now all the colours of the rainbow,
and pronouncing himself satisfied with it.

'The swelling is going down nicely,' he said, probing
the joint with gentle fingers. 'Another few days and you

may get up—I'll bring crutches with me when the time comes.' He opened his bag. 'You are sleeping, Mrs Macdonald?'

She gave a grudging assent as he took out his stethoscope. 'I'll just go over your chest,' he explained and, at her look of surprise, added smoothly, 'it is usual after a fall such as you have had, it may take a day or so before the shock of it wears off.'

He took her blood-pressure too, and although Rosie watched his face closely she could detect no change in its calm blandness.

Dr Cameron didn't hurry away, but stood leaning against the door, his hands in the pockets of his elderly and excellently tailored tweed jacket, listening to Mrs Macdonald's tetchy opinions of modern youth, fast food and microwave ovens. He gave her his full attention, and they parted, if not the best of friends, at least on speaking terms.

Rosie, intent on getting him alone, followed him out of the room. 'I want a word with you,' she told him urgently, 'if you can spare a moment.'

His, 'of course,' was non-committal as he followed her down to the lounge, crowded with frustrated anglers and walkers because of the heavy rain. They found a table jammed up against a wall, and ordered coffee, and she began without preamble.

'How soon can Grandmother go home? Could we get an ambulance or a car to take her to Edinburgh? She has a daughter living with her, and a splendid housekeeper, and I could arrange for a nurse if you think it necessary.' At his faintly surprised look, she added, 'I sound as if I want to get rid of her, don't I? But, you

see, I have a job at home, and I have to be back by the
end of next week...'

Their coffee came, and she poured out and handed
him a cup.

'As far as the ankle is concerned there is no reason
why Mrs Macdonald should not be taken back to her
home. Unfortunately there is a complication. She has a
heart condition, and the shock of the fall has made it
worse. Rest in bed is absolutely necessary for several
more days—even a week. Her blood-pressure is far too
high, and she is not by nature a calm person, is she? A
placid life is essential to her well-being. Ideally she should
stay where she is. Perhaps the housekeeper or your aunt
could come here and take your place?'

'Then she would want to know why...'

'Indeed, yes. Is your job very important to you? Do
you stand a risk of losing it if you were to stay on here?'

She nodded and said, 'yes,' slowly, thinking that her
mother would miss her share of the household expenses
until she could find another job. Messrs Crabbe, Crabbe
and Twitchett, a young, rather pushy firm, would show
no compunction in finding someone to replace her.
Shorthand typists were quite thick on the ground.

She said out loud, 'But of course I'll stay.' She gave
him a direct look. 'She is my granny.'

'Good, but I think that we must establish some sort
of routine. You must have some leisure during the day.
Do you get enough sleep?'

'Well, Granny takes quite a time to settle, and she
wakes early and likes a cup of tea and then goes to sleep
again.'

'So it is essential that you should have a few hours
each day to yourself. I suggest that you settle her for a

rest after lunch, arrange for her to have her tea, and return to her around five or six o'clock. I dare say there is a sensible chambermaid who would undertake to cast an eye over your grandmother from time to time and give her tea.'

'I did come to Scotland especially to be her companion on the train trip...'

'Indeed, but not to nurse her for twenty-four hours of the day and night for a week or more.'

Dr Cameron smiled suddenly at her, and just for a moment she liked him very much.

'Get through today, and tomorrow I will have a talk with her. Now I must go—I have someone to see at the youth hostel at Loch Ossian.'

He lifted a finger for the bill, wished her goodbye, and left the hotel.

Rosie went back to the invalid presently, and read the *Daily Telegraph* from end to end before lunch, and after that meal, since her grandmother declared that she needed her company, sat quietly while the old lady talked. Mostly about her youth and the early years of her marriage and, when that topic was exhausted, politics and the shortcomings of the younger generation.

Mercifully tea gave her pause, and Rosie produced a pack of cards and suggested Patience before being allowed to go down to the dining-room for her dinner. There was still an hour or so before bedtime, and Mrs Macdonald, far from being tired, became chatty.

'Quite a pleasant man, Dr Cameron,' she allowed. 'I am inclined to take his advice. He is not so young, and must have had some experience. Is he Dr Finlay's partner, I wonder? There surely can't be enough work for the pair of them.'

'It's a scattered practice,' said Rosie, and stifled a yawn, not caring in the least where the man came from.

Her grandmother gave her a sharp glance. 'Married, do you suppose?'

'I've no idea, Granny. I should think that very likely he is; he's not young.'

Her grandmother spoke with a snap. 'Not a day over thirty-five, I should imagine. You're not so young yourself, Rosie.'

The kind of remark which made it hard for Rosie to love her Granny as she ought.

She had to admire Dr Cameron's tactics the next morning. He was later than usual, and he looked tired. But he was as immaculate as usual, and just as impersonally pleasant, reassuring Mrs Macdonald that she was making a steady progress, explaining that the longer she stayed in bed off her foot, the sooner she would be able to walk without pain.

'Another few days,' he warned her, 'and then I will see about getting you home. You are making the most remarkable recovery.'

Mrs Macdonald gave a smug smile. 'I pride myself upon my fortitude and common sense,' she told him.

It was an easy step from there to point out that Rosie, if she were to give her grandmother her full attention, should take necessary exercise.

'If I might suggest,' said Dr Cameron at his most urbane, 'two or three hours in the fresh air each afternoon? I am sure that there is a chambermaid able to bring you your tea and answer your bell, but I hope that for your own good you will rest quietly after your lunch. Shall you be willing to try this for a day or so? Now that you are feeling so much better I dare say you have been thinking along these lines yourself.'

To Rosie's astonishment her grandmother replied quite sharply that of course she had.

'Then that is settled, if—er—Rosie feels able, there are some splendid walks around the hotel.'

Of which she was well aware, although she had no intention of saying so. She still didn't like him, she told herself, but she had to admit that he was doing his best for her.

He went away presently giving her a casual nod. 'I'll be in tomorrow—I have to pass the hotel.'

She accompanied him down to the foyer, and as he went he said, 'Be sure and get out for a walk each day.' He stopped unexpectedly so that she almost tripped up. 'You're not very happy, are you?' he asked, but didn't wait for an answer.

'A good thing, too,' muttered Rosie crossly, 'for it's none of his business.'

The new regime worked well; her grandmother offered no opposition when, having settled her for her afternoon nap, she got into her gilet and sensible shoes, reassured her that she had warned the chambermaid, rearranged the pillows, adjusted the window curtains to her grandmother's taste, and at last took herself off.

She took the road towards Loch Tulla, walking briskly. It was a fine afternoon, but it wouldn't last—the sky above Ben Dorian behind her was ominously grey, but she didn't care; to be out walking in well-remembered country was enough to make her happy. That evening, she reflected, she would phone her mother and tell her that nothing had changed in the wild and lonely countryside around her. Just for a little while she was blissfully happy, and some of the happiness was still with her when she returned to soothe a disgruntled grandparent who declared that she had been bored, in pain, and neglected.

'Kirsty came to see you,' said Rosie. 'I met her as I came in, and she said that you had had a long nap and a splendid tea.'

She wished she hadn't repeated that, for her grandmother declared loudly that no servant was to be trusted. 'Of course if you wish to disbelieve your own kith and kin...'

It took her the rest of the evening to coax Mrs Macdonald into a good frame of mind again.

When Dr Cameron came in the morning she half expected her grandmother to object to being left on her own in the afternoon, and she couldn't help but admire his handling of her recalcitrant grandparent so that grudging permission was given once more with the rider that it was to be hoped that the state of affairs wouldn't last.

'Just as soon as you are fit to be moved, Mrs Macdonald,' said the doctor, at his most soothing, 'I will arrange your return home. You are doing splendidly, due largely to your co-operation and fortitude.'

Rosie, watching the old lady's pleased smile at that, thought Dr Cameron was a cunning rascal, obviously used to getting his own way once he had made up his mind.

Beyond a civil good day as he went he had nothing to say to her, which rather annoyed her. Even if she didn't like him their barbed conversation made her day more interesting.

Two more days went by, and Rosie's lovely face took on a healthy glow from the energetic walks she took each day. It was a pity that the weather was changing; there was more persistent rain and a strengthening wind—hardly a day for a tramp—but Dr Cameron had said that morning that her grandmother was well enough to return home, and this might be her last chance to take a last look ... She borrowed an old mac from one of the maids, tied her head in a scarf, assured her grandmother, with not a vestige of truth, that the weather was clearing, and left the hotel.

The steady drizzle didn't bother her, nor did the great gusts of wind. The sky was leaden and the mountains loomed, grey and forbidding, but she had been brought up in surroundings such as these, and wasn't deterred from her resolve to walk as far as possible towards Rannoch Moor. She had no hope of actually getting there, but at least she would be able to reach its very edge. She would walk for an hour and then turn back.

The hour was almost up and she was a good four miles from the hotel when the drizzle turned to torrential rain. There was no escaping it; she was on a lonely stretch of road bordered by coarse grass and last year's bracken, patterned with the vivid green of the new growth. The low-lying shrubs offered no shelter, and there was nothing to do but turn round and walk back. She paused to wipe the rain from her face with an already sopping hanky, and didn't hear the Land Rover come to a halt on the other side of the road. Its door opened and Dr Cameron roared, 'Over here, Rosie, and look sharp about it!'

She sloshed across the road, her shoes full of water, relieved to see him, and at the same time vexed that he

should bawl at her in such a fashion. He had the door
open, and she climbed in and squelched into the seat
beside him, and he drove off, far too fast she considered, before she had fastened her seatbelt. She mopped
her face, glad that she would be back soon.

'An emergency?' she asked, and when he didn't do
more than grunt, 'Thank you for picking me up, I'll be
glad to get out of these wet clothes.'

They were approaching Bridge of Orchy; she could
see the hotel, standing back from the station and the
road. A cup of tea and a hot bath would be more than
welcome. She gave a sigh of relief which turned to a
surprised gasp as he drove down a side-road which joined
the road to Oban.

'Sorry I can't stop,' said Dr Cameron in what she considered to be a heartless manner. The next minute she
felt ashamed of herself; what were hot baths and cups
of tea compared with emergencies?

She peered through the driving rain as he turned off
the road on to a narrow country lane running through
fir trees. She knew the lane, for it was within a few miles
of her old home. They would pass close to Inverard
unless he turned off again, and side-roads were few and
far between.

He didn't turn off, but presently raced through an open
gateway and slowed then because the drive was steep and
narrow and winding.

'Why are you coming here?' She strove to keep her
voice quiet.

'Dr Finlay is out on a case. The medical men at Oban
are tied up—I got a call on the car phone.'

They had reached the end of the drive, and the house
came into view. It hadn't changed—white walls, gables,

tall chimneys, shallow steps to the wide front door standing ajar, sitting cosily within its circle of trees and gardens, facing the mountains across a wide grass meadow.

She gave a small sigh, and he turned to look at her.

'Know this place? Who lives here? I was only given the address...'

'Macdonald,' and at his sudden understanding look, 'I was born here. Donald Macdonald is my uncle.'

He had the doors open. 'Out you get and inside with you, and don't waste my time. You can dry off somewhere...'

He mounted the steps and went into the square hall with doors on all sides. One of them opened now, and a small elderly woman in a flowered pinny came to meet them.

'The doctor—thank God for that. He's in the drawing-room, we've not dared to move him.' Her eyes lighted on Rosie, and her face broke into a wide smile. 'Miss Rosie—in with ye, lassie, while I take the doctor along.'

The doctor had cast down his Burberry and followed the woman through the door, and Rosie stopped to take off her mac and headscarf, and made haste to follow. Nothing had changed, she saw that at a glance as she crossed the charming room to the vast sofa where her uncle lay.

'Is there anything I can do?' She looked at the unconscious face of her uncle, and felt a pang of pity; he had treated her father with unkindness and she had never liked him, but now he lay, a lonely elderly man with no wife and no family to be with him.

'Open my bag and get out the syringe in a plastic envelope, the small bottle with spirit written on it, and one of the woollen swabs beside it. Put them where I can reach them, and get someone to get a bed ready.'

He didn't look at her; he was bending over his patient, listening to his chest, so she did exactly as she had been told and then, leaving Mrs MacFee with him, hurried through to the dining-room through the open archway and up the small second staircase leading from it. Old Robert, the odd-job man, and a young girl with a tear-stained face were standing in the doorway leading to the kitchen, and Rosie said, 'Come up with me, will you, and help me get a bed ready?'

Her uncle's room was at the front of the house; if he was to be carried upstairs, then it would be easier if they used the main staircase in the inner hall leading up from the drawing-room. Rosie ran through the passages and opened the door wide. 'We'd better take the bedclothes off.' She gave the girl a reassuring smile. 'What is your name?'

'Flora, miss, I'm the housemaid.'

'Well, Flora, would you switch on the lights? And I should think one pillow would do.' She frowned. 'Perhaps you'd better fetch several more, though, for I'm not sure if Mr Macdonald should sit up or not.'

She gave a quick look round, moved a bedside table to make it easier to reach the bed, and said, 'I'm going downstairs again to tell the doctor to use the main staircase.'

Dr Cameron was still bending over her uncle. He didn't look up as she went in, but said in his calm way, 'Is the bed ready?' and when she said 'yes' he lifted his patient with apparent ease.

'Lead the way...'

She went ahead, turning every few steps to make sure that the doctor was all right. 'Pillow?' she asked urgently as they reached the bedroom.

'One,' Dr Cameron laid his patient on the bed. He was breathing rather fast, but that was all. He must be all of fifteen stone, reflected Rosie and, being a practical young woman, began to ease off her uncle's shoes.

Her uncle was still unconscious.

'We will get him undressed,' stated the doctor. 'Trousers and jacket, leave everything else.'

When that was done he turned to Rosie and said, 'Go and telephone the hotel, reassure your grandmother. Will it upset her to be told?'

'She hasn't spoken to Uncle Donald since he came here to live, but I'd rather not tell her—not yet, anyway.'

'Tell her what you think is best, and then come back here.'

She was still wringing wet and with no hope of getting dry, at least for the moment. When she got downstairs she kicked off her shoes, stripped off her tights, and went to the telephone. It took a minute or two to explain to the manager where she was and why.

'If you could tell my grandmother,' she asked, 'that I am quite safe, and will be back just as soon as Dr Cameron can leave his patient.'

Mrs MacFee was at her elbow as she put down the phone.

'You'll get these wet things off you, Miss Rosie. Ye can sit in my dressing-gown while they dry—it'll take but a wee while.'

'I can't just yet, Mrs MacFee, the doctor might need help.' She raced back upstairs, and the housekeeper, tutting indignantly, went back to the kitchen to warm up the soup she was sure would be needed.

'A fine, strong lass,' she grumbled at Old Robert. 'It won't be my fault if she catches her death of cold—and why should she be here after all this time and them not speaking, her father and him?' She nodded her head towards the ceiling. 'That's a braw man, that doctor. Fetch in some more peat, Robert, will you? The fire'll need banking for the night.'

'Woman, it's but five o'clock.'

'And a long night ahead of us, Robert.'

'Stay here, will you?' asked Dr Cameron as Rosie reached the bedroom. 'I've some phoning to do. No need to do anything, but give a yell if he comes round.'

She sat down close to the bed, her eyes glued to her uncle's unconscious face. It was quiet in the room save for his slow breaths, so quiet that she had to strain her ears to hear them. It seemed an age before the doctor came soft-footed through the half-open door. He said nothing, checked his patient's pulse once more, and then sat down on the other side of the bed.

Presently he looked across at her.

'Go down and get those wet things off; your Mrs MacFee is seething with anxiety for fear you will catch cold. Then come back here—I might need you.'

He could have been giving orders to a nurse on a hospital ward. Polite, impersonal, and quite sure he would be obeyed.

She did as she was told, and didn't say a word. In the kitchen she was given a scalding cup of tea, and was told to go up the back stairs to Mrs MacFee's room, strip off her clothes, and put on the dressing-gown she would find behind the door. It was a voluminous garment, very woolly, and she wrapped it around her person with a sigh of relief as Mrs MacFee came trotting in with her tights.

'You put these on, my lass, and button up that gown all the way down. Come and sit in the kitchen by the fire—your things will dry in no time.'

'I'm to go back upstairs,' Rosie insisted.

'Like that? Whatever next...?'

'He's a doctor, Mrs MacFee,' said Rosie. 'He's concerned with Uncle Donald—I could be there with nothing on at all and he wouldn't notice!'

She gave the elderly cheek a quick kiss, nipped through the upstairs passages, and slid into the room without a word.

If the doctor noticed her appearance he gave no sign. 'He is regaining consciousness. Sit where he can see you.

So she sat close to the bed again, and sure enough her uncle's eyelids soon fluttered and opened. He closed them again at once, and then after a minute opened them again. 'Rosie?' His voice was a thread of sound.

'Yes, Uncle.'

'Strange you're here—I've been thinking about you...your father...' He closed his eyes again, and she looked at the doctor, who looked calmly back at her and didn't speak.

'Never liked me much, did you?' went on the weary voice. 'Kicked me when I beat that dog. Sorry about that. So long ago. I've been a fool.'

Rosie took one of his hands in hers. 'That's all over and done with, Uncle... The doctor's here, you were taken ill.'

The tired face turned slowly on the pillow. 'Don't know you. Married to Rosie, are you?'

Dr Cameron looked faintly amused. 'Indeed not. Your own doctor was out on a case, and I got your house-keeper's message on the car phone. Dr Douglas will be with us very shortly and it is to be hoped that you can be taken to hospital in Oban as soon as you are fit enough to move.'

The man in the bed closed his eyes again, and presently the doctor said quietly to Rosie, 'Go and get some clothes on.'

'You'll be all right?' She went pink the moment she had spoken. It had been a silly remark; she didn't need his slow smile to let her know that.

When she got back there was another man there. Dr Douglas—a youngish man who had taken over old Dr MacTavish's practice during the last year. It surprised her that he deferred to Dr Cameron's opinion; she supposed that it was because he was a good deal younger.

Her uncle was recovering slowly. The two men examined him together, and Dr Douglas went away to telephone.

While he was gone Dr Cameron said, 'We shall send your uncle to hospital. He needs urgent treatment. As soon as the ambulance is here and he is gone I'll take you back.'

Which, after an hour or so, he did. Mrs MacFee had insisted on hot soup for them both, and ten minutes by the blazing fire, and had taken the opportunity of discovering just why Rosie was there before they were allowed to get into the Land Rover and drive away. The ambulance had come and gone, and Dr Douglas had driven away behind it with the promise that he would be sure and let them know how the patient did.

It was after ten o'clock when they left at last; the rain had settled down to a soft drizzle with patches of mist. Here and there the road was awash, and it was hard to see more than a few yards ahead, but the doctor remained unperturbed, and Rosie was too tired to bother. He drew up before the hotel entrance, got out, and opened her door.

'I'll let you have any news when I see your grandmother in the morning,' he promised. 'Now go to bed as quickly as you can.'

He put a finger under her chin and kissed her gently.

'Rather an eventful day,' he added, and pushed her gently through the door.

CHAPTER THREE

IT WOULD be prudent to get out of her still damp clothes
before she went to see if her grandmother was still awake,
Rosie decided. She was greeted with sympathy by the
head waiter, who offered to get her something to eat.

'Oh, that really would be kind, I'm famished.' Her
eyes strayed to the clock. 'Heavens, it's after ten o'clock!
A sandwich would do, and a pot of tea please, and could
it possibly be brought to my room? I'm so wet still, and
I must get out of my things.'

'Leave it to me, Miss Macdonald.' He was a kindly
man, and a little sorry for her, tied to the old lady for
hours and hours on end.

In her room she got into her dressing-gown, and
peeped into her grandmother's room. The old lady was
sitting up in bed reading, but she put the book down
when she saw Rosie.

'Where have you been?' she demanded peevishly, 'You
ungrateful girl, jaunting off in that fashion, leaving me
alone among strangers.'

Rosie, longing for a hot bath and a large pot of tea,
pulled her dressing-gown more closely around her.

'I went for a walk, Granny,' she began patiently. 'It
rained—very hard—Dr Cameron came by in his Land
Rover and gave me a lift, only he couldn't stop because
he was going to an emergency.'

Her grandmother uttered a sound which could have
been 'pish' or 'tush', indicative of her disbelief.

'Rubbish, of course he could have stopped here. I have never heard such nonsense! I suppose you wanted to spend the afternoon with him?'

Rosie giggled, sneezed, and then blew her pretty nose. 'Granny, we don't like each other. He's the last person I would want to spend an afternoon with, and I'm sure he feels the same. Only one wouldn't leave one's worst enemy to walk miles in such a downpour.'

Her grandmother said, 'Huh! So where was this dire emergency?'

Rosie sneezed again. It had to be said. 'Inverard, Granny. Uncle Donald.'

Mrs Macdonald said quickly, 'Well, I don't want to hear about it. Now you're here you can pour me some of that lemonade and do my pillows. I suppose I'd better have one of those pills Dr Cameron sent. You had better go to bed yourself, Rosie, and let us have no more traipsing around. I must say I expected more consideration from you.'

Rosie considered answering this, and decided not to. She fetched the pill and the lemonade, arranged the pillows just so, switched off the lights except for the small bedside lamp, kissed her grandmother goodnight, and went thankfully back to her room. Someone had put a tray there—a plate of toasted sandwiches, cheese and biscuits, a bowl of yoghurt and a large pot of tea. She ran the bath, bore the tray into the bathroom, set it on a stool by the bath, and lay in its comforting heat while she demolished everything on the tray. There was a small glass of brandy lurking behind the teapot; she prudently saved it until she was curled up in bed before she tossed it off. She wasn't in the habit of drinking brandy; she spluttered and choked, aware of its comforting warmth before she fell instantly asleep.

Mrs Macdonald was still tetchy in the morning, and since she had nothing more to say about Rosie's absence the previous day Rosie said nothing as well. After breakfast she helped her grandmother into a chair and settled the injured limb on a stool, and awaited the arrival of Dr Cameron. She felt heavy-eyed and out of sorts, and from time to time, to her grandmother's annoyance, she sneezed.

The doctor arrived at his usual hour, immaculate in his elderly tweeds, looking in the very best of health. Rosie wished him a rather cold, terse good morning, and sneezed again.

'A little under the weather?' he wanted to know kindly. 'I'll let you have something to check that cold—nasty things, colds.'

He had spoken blandly, but he was amused, too. She frowned heavily at him. 'Thank you, it's nothing—just a summer cold. I don't need anything for it.'

'You will take whatever Dr Cameron gives you, Rosie,' said her grandmother. 'You may be a great, healthy girl, but if I were to become infected it might be a serious matter.'

Rosie didn't reply; to be described as a great, healthy girl did nothing for her ego. She avoided the doctor's eye, and with a slightly heightened colour turned back the light shawl which shrouded the injured ankle.

'Very nice,' he pronounced presently. 'Tomorrow you shall try walking with the crutches I shall bring with me. I think that you might make arrangements to go home within the next few days. Do you have a car, Mrs Macdonald?'

'Certainly not. If necessary I hire a car and a chauffeur. Why do you ask?'

'I shall be going to Edinburgh on Saturday; I can offer you and Rosie a lift.' He noticed Rosie's questioning look. 'Not in the Land Rover.'

Mrs Macdonald wasn't exactly mean, but she didn't believe in spending money on something which could be obtained without it. She accepted with alacrity. 'You have a practice in Edinburgh?' she wanted to know.

'Yes. You have made a splendid recovery, Mrs Macdonald. I will write a note to your doctor and give him details.'

'Oh, but I wish you to attend me until my ankle is quite healed.'

'I can hardly do that, Mrs Macdonald. I'm sure that you will be quite satisfied with your doctor's treatment if any is needed.'

'In that case I shall expect you to visit me—not professionally.'

'I shall be delighted to do so...'

He was interrupted by one of Rosie's sneezes, and he turned round to look at her.

'I think I must deal with that before it gets too severe.' He opened his bag and shook out some tablets. 'Take one now and then four-hourly. I'll bring enough for the full treatment when I come tomorrow.'

He had bidden them goodbye and was almost at the door when Mrs Macdonald asked, 'Donald Macdonald—is he dead?'

'No; there is very little to be done, however. He has a history of heart trouble. I'm sorry, Mrs Macdonald.'

'I haven't set eyes on him for years. He didn't deal fairly with Rosie's father...' Her voice held no feeling.

Rosie remembered the lonely figure on the sofa.

'Granny, please...' She bustled the doctor through the door and shut it firmly on her grandmother.

'She doesn't mean it,' she told him. 'She's old.'

He stood looking down at her. 'Yes. Do your parents wish to be informed?'

'Oh, yes. They haven't seen Uncle Donald for a long time—not since we left Inverard. They have never spoken of him, though they have never borne him a grudge. I think that they might like to know how he is. Granny will be furious; you see, she can't forgive him, not even now...'

'Why don't you phone now?'

He swept her willy-nilly down the stairs, and picked up the telephone on the reception desk.

'An urgent call,' he said blandly, and stood beside her while she dialled.

Her mother answered. 'Darling,' she began before Rosie could get a word in edgeways, 'you have to be back at your job on Monday. Will you be able to get here by then?'

Rosie drew a deep breath and explained.

'Oh, dear? said her mother when Rosie paused. 'The poor man—not that I like him, but one has to be sorry... What kind of man is this Dr Cameron?'

'Just a doctor, Mother,' said Rosie evasively, aware that he was standing beside her, listening to every word. 'Will you tell Father? And I'll let you know how Uncle Donald is. And will you let them know at the office, please?' She paused to think. 'Once Granny is back home I should be able to come home straight away.'

'That will be Sunday or Monday?'

'Yes, I hope so. I'll ring you again tomorrow.'

She put down the receiver as several people came in through the hotel entrance; the Royal Scotsman was in the station, and the train manager and the two stewards, as well as the guide, had come to visit her grandmother.

'I'll leave you,' said Dr Cameron, and was gone before she could say goodbye.

It was nice to see their cheerful faces and hear their friendly voices. They had flowers and fruit with them, and Rosie took them upstairs to her grandmother before going in search of someone to bring coffee to her room. They couldn't stay long; Jamie had to go almost at once, as the coach was taking the passengers on the scheduled trip, and the other three had to go again after half an hour, since the train was due to leave.

Rosie was sorry to see them go; she had liked them all, and they had been more than kind and thoughtful.

'I'll come again,' she promised, 'but I don't know when.'

They hugged her in turn, bade Mrs Macdonald a more dignified farewell, and hurried back to the train. A brief visit, but it supplied a topic of conversation for the rest of the morning. Her grandmother, reflected Rosie, hadn't mentioned Uncle Donald once.

Her leisure that afternoon was brief; Mrs Macdonald, now that she had her crutches, intended to waste no time in becoming an expert in their use, which meant that Rosie had to be there to give help when needed, and when her grandmother was tired she insisted that Rosie should start to repack their cases.

'There's still a whole day, Granny,' Rosie pointed out.

'You have nothing better to do,' the old lady remarked. 'You may just as well occupy yourself usefully as moon around out of doors.'

Dr Cameron was late the next morning. He gave no reason for it, though, merely took another look at the ankle, watched his patient on her crutches, pronounced her fit to go home to the care of her own doctor, and reminded them that he would call for them about ten o'clock on the day after tomorrow.

He enquired after Rosie's cold, and went again after the briefest of visits. He hadn't mentioned Uncle Donald; Rosie, with a muttered excuse to her grandmother, ran down the stairs after him, and caught him up as he was going through the hotel entrance.

'Uncle Donald. Is he any better?'

He paused on the step. 'He is conscious—in Intensive Care—but I think it unlikely that he will recover.' He stared down at her thoughtfully. 'Do you wish to see him?'

'There isn't anyone else...'

'No. I'll take you to the hospital tomorrow morning.'

'Granny...' she began.

'Leave her to me, just be ready.'

After the stormy weather the day was fine and Rosie longed to be out of doors, but there was little chance of that; she repacked, and read the *Daily Telegraph* from end to end as usual, perambulated to and fro with her grandmother on her crutches and, while the old lady slept, did her nails and washed her hair, all the while wondering if she was doing the wise thing in visiting the hospital to see her uncle. Dr Cameron had said that he wasn't likely to recover, and he had no family now.

Dr Cameron came earlier than usual; he sat down as though he had the whole morning in which to do nothing, listening to her grandmother giving forceful opinions about this, that and the other, and only when the old lady had talked herself into a good mood did he observe casually that it might be a good idea if Rosie were to get some fresh air. 'I'll take her with me.'

He smiled charmingly at her, and turned to Rosie.

'Ready? It's rather a splendid morning. I'm going over to the youth hostel; you can take a stroll while I'm there—it will help to shake off that cold.'

He swept Rosie away before her grandmother could make any objection, urged her into the Land Rover, and drove away.

'Are you really going to the youth hostel?'

'Of course, I have to deliver some tablets on Dr Finlay's behalf.'

Her nod was friendly and he drove in silence for quite a time, but presently said, 'I shall be all of five minutes there. We will go on to Ballachullish and down to Oban; it's the long way round, but quicker than turning back.'

He gave her a faintly smiling glance. 'Not that I am in a hurry.'

'Well, if you're sure you can spare the time.' She settled back to enjoy the drive.

They stopped just outside Oban at a small hotel, and had coffee before driving on to the town and the hospital. Donald Macdonald was still in Intensive Care, but since Dr Cameron seemed to be known by everyone they encountered as they went through the hospital entrance, and Dr Douglas came to meet them, there was no objection to Rosie's visiting him.

'He's not too good,' said Dr Douglas, leading the way, 'but he's conscious. He'll be glad to see you.'

Rosie wasn't sure about that. She greeted her uncle quietly and with caution; he might take umbrage at the sight of her, and that would do him no good at all. She remembered his sudden surges of temper. But here, she saw at once, was a man who had no temper left in him; he was too ill.

She sat down by his bed, taking care to avoid the various tubes and portable machines encircling it.

He managed a smile. 'Coals of fire, Rosie?'

'No, Uncle. But Father and Mother will want to know how you are getting on when I go home. I phoned them—they hope you will feel better soon.'

'I find that hard to believe,' he whispered.

'True, all the same. I'm going home on Monday, Father will phone the hospital each day.' She caught Dr Douglas's glance and got up.

'I mustn't make you tired.' She squeezed the hand she had been holding. 'Get better soon.'

Dr Cameron was standing quietly behind her; she was surprised to see that he had taken off his car coat, and had a stethoscope swinging from one hand. There was a ward sister too, as well as Dr Douglas.

'I shan't be long,' said Dr Cameron. 'Wait in Sister's office, will you?'

He opened the door for her, polite and faintly impatient for her to be gone.

Later, once more in the Land Rover, she said, 'Everyone knew you there—have you a practice in Oban?'

'No. I go to the hospital occasionally.'

He had answered her coolly, but she persisted. 'The landlord at the hotel said that you were staying at Dr Finlay's...'

'He was quite right. There is some splendid fishing hereabouts. You must know that.'

Which didn't answer her question, and made it difficult to pursue the subject. She said with something of a snap, 'Uncle Donald is in good hands—I like Dr Douglas.'

'He would be glad to know that; he's taken a fancy to you—you could do worse, he's got a good practice and should go far...'

Rosie's bosom swelled with indignation. 'Well, really whatever will you say next?' She paused to take breath and he added carelessly,

'He's not married?'

She ground splendid teeth. 'You're awful—I've never met a man like you...'

'I'm glad to hear that.'

'Are you married?' She hadn't meant to speak her thoughts out loud, but once said there was no taking it back.

'Er—no. But I'm hopeful of being so in the not too distant future.'

For some reason his answer depressed her. Vaguely she supposed that she was sorry for the girl. Before they came to open warfare she supposed that she should change the conversation.

'What a pleasant morning,' she observed in a polite voice which would have frozen a kettle of boiling water.

The doctor gave a bellow of laughter. 'Are you burying the hatchet or offering an olive branch? I'll settle for either, at least let us part on speaking terms.'

They were almost at the hotel, and he went on casually, 'I'll be here at ten o'clock tomorrow if that suits you and Mrs Macdonald?'

'Oh, yes. We can be ready by then. You're quite sure it's convenient? We're not taking up your time?'

'Not in the least. I did tell you that I have to be in Edinburgh tomorrow.'

He stopped the car and got out, and went to open her door.

'Thank you for taking me,' she said frostily, 'I'm very grateful.'

He nodded, and stood watching her until she had gone inside and then got back into the Land Rover and drove himself away.

Rosie, sneaking a quick backward look at him from inside the door, could see that he was smiling. It puzzled her, for she had not said anything to amuse him.

Back with her grandmother she assured that lady that she had had a very pleasant drive.

'I can see that; you have quite a good colour—there is nothing like exercise in the fresh air,' remarked Mrs Macdonald, who seldom ventured into the outdoors.

Rosie forebore from telling her that the colour was the result of her vexatious conversation with Dr Cameron, and offered to accompany her down the corridor outside the bedroom on her daily exercise with her crutches.

'We are to be ready by ten o'clock in the morning,' she reminded her grandmother. 'I'll order your breakfast a little earlier, shall I? So that you don't have to hurry.'

'I suppose we shouldn't keep him waiting.'

'Well, I don't think so—doctors usually have a busy day, don't they?'

They were ready by ten o'clock; Rosie had prudently allowed time for paying the bill, saying their goodbyes, and making sure that their luggage was in the foyer so that when Dr Cameron arrived they were waiting for him.

His good morning was brisk; obviously he had no time to stand about passing the time of day. He helped Mrs Macdonald down the steps, and Rosie and the porter with their cases followed.

The car parked at the bottom of the steps wasn't what she had expected—a dark blue Rolls-Royce.

Her grandmother had stopped at the car doors.

'How very kind,' she observed in her commanding voice, 'to consider my comfort and hire a car in which I can travel without being jarred and jolted.'

The doctor was stowing the crutches in the boot, and didn't look up. 'I think you will be comfortable enough. I'll help you into the back seat; there is a cushion for your foot.' He glanced up. 'Rosie, get in front, will you?'

A good many of the hotel staff had come out to see them off. Mrs Macdonald waved in a regal fashion, pronounced herself as comfortable as it was possible to be, and expressed the hope that the journey wouldn't take too long.

'Two hours, perhaps a little more. We will go down on the A82, by-pass Glasgow, and join the motorway to Edinburgh.'

He took the A819, going south, drove round the head of Loch Fyne, and joined the A82 running alongside Loch Lomond. He drove fast, and beyond an enquiry as to his passengers' comfort had little to say.

The journey was half done before Rosie plucked up the courage to say, 'We simply cannot allow you to bear the expense of hiring this car. I'm afraid we didn't think about it, but if you will let us know...'

'I'm on good terms with the owner; there's no question of paying.'

'Oh, well, that's very good of your friend to let us travel in it.' She glanced at his rather stern profile. 'You're not—that is, it's really so?'

He turned to look at her down his handsome nose. 'I am not in the habit of having my word questioned.'

'No, no. I'm sure you're not,' said Rosie soothingly. 'I just wondered. I'm sorry if I ruffled you.'

'Neither do I ruffle easily.'

They went almost the length of Loch Lomond before he spoke again.

'You are glad to be going home?'

In her mind's eye she saw the remote majesty of the Highlands, the towering black mountains, the waterfalls, the bracken, the heather and the breathtaking beauty of it all.

'I shall be glad to see my mother and father,' she told him.

That was true, only she was leaving her thoughts and her heart at Inverard. She wondered what would happen to the house if her uncle were to die. There were remote cousins on his side of the family, but they had lived for years in Canada, and would hardly wish to uproot themselves.

'You will fly back?' he asked idly.

'Perhaps, in a day or two. I believe Granny has made some arrangements with her own doctor—I don't know if she has to go to hospital. If so, I'd better stay until that's seen to.'

He made a non-committal reply, and began a casual conversation about the country they were driving through. They joined the motorway shortly, and on the outskirts of Glasgow he turned south to avoid the city's heart, and picked up the motorway on its eastern outskirts. It was barely forty miles to Edinburgh on the M8, it took that number of minutes to reach the city, and when Rosie offered directions Dr Cameron said, 'It's all right, I know my way.' And very shortly after he drew up before Mrs Macdonald's door.

Elspeth had the door open before they were out of the car, with Aunt Carrie peering over her shoulder, getting in each other's way while the doctor lifted Mrs Macdonald out of the car and carried her up the steps.

She was received with a good deal of fuss while he returned to the car to fetch the crutches and the luggage. Rosie had hung back a little so that Aunt Carrie and Elspeth could make much of her grandmother, but she took the crutches from the doctor so that he could deal with their cases, and ushered him into the house.

He said pleasantly, 'Let everyone see how well you walk again, Mrs Macdonald,' and handed the crutches to her with a smile.

Mrs Macdonald was at her most gracious. 'Let me introduce you—my daughter, Caroline, and Elspeth, our housekeeper. This is Dr Cameron who has so kindly driven us back and looked after me so well. Rosie, go with Elspeth and bring coffee to the drawing-room.'

'I must be on my way, Mrs Macdonald. If I might give Rosie one or two last-minute instructions until your doctor calls...?'

'Well, I suppose that you are a busy man. Rosie, go into the dining-room with the doctor. I shall go to the drawing-room; come there when you are ready to go.'

In the gloomy dining-room Rosie asked, 'Should I stay longer? I've arranged to go home on Tuesday.'

'No need to stay. The sooner your grandmother starts gentle walking the better. Her own doctor will be round to see her, will he not? I think it likely that she will be able to manage with a stick within a very short time.'

He smiled suddenly. 'It hasn't been quite the holiday you expected, has it?'

'Well, no, but it was lovely to see Inverard again.' She sighed without knowing she did so. 'Thank you for bringing us back, it was very kind. Are you sure you won't have coffee before you go?'

'I've things to do, I'm afraid.' He held out a large hand and engulfed hers. 'It is a great pity that we need to part when we are beginning to be friends.'

'Oh, are we?' She went rather pink. 'Well, yes, perhaps... You will want to say goodbye to Granny...'

Mrs Macdonald was sitting in an upright chair, intent on telling her daughter every detail of her mishap. 'You are going, Doctor? I shall tell Dr MacLeod how very helpful you have been. You are sure that I shall be all right on the stairs? I managed very well at the motel for the last day or so, but I am nervous...'

'Don't be, Mrs Macdonald, you are perfectly safe, only don't put your weight on that foot until your doctor says you may.'

He shook hands with her and with Carrie, said goodbye, and Rosie went into the hall to see him out. Elspeth was already there, waiting to see him out of the door, so she said lamely, 'Well, goodbye, Doctor,' and watched him go, surprised at the regret she felt at the sight of his vast back disappearing into the street.

Dr MacLeod came to see them later that afternoon, pronounced himself very satisfied with the ankle, and said that he had made arrangements for Mrs Macdonald to go the Royal Infirmary on Monday morning.

'For an X-ray,' he assured her. 'Nothing to be alarmed about. If it is satisfactory you won't need those crutches, just a stout stick. The appointment is for ten o'clock. I shall see you there.'

Mrs Macdonald was enjoying being the centre of attention. She was accustomed to being the most important person in the house, anyway; now she basked in the sympathetic attention she was getting. She recounted every detail of each day since they had set out on the train together, with her opinion about the hotel, the train, its staff, the weather and the food. It took the rest of the day, and she never once mentioned Uncle Donald. Rosie wondered if she should tell Aunt Carrie, and decided not to—for the moment, at any rate.

Only when their combined efforts had got her grandmother up the stairs and into bed, and she and Aunt Carrie were having a cup of tea before going to their own beds did she ask, 'Did you have a good time, Aunt Carrie? Go out at all?'

Her companion blushed. 'Oh, Rosie, dear, I did... You can't imagine... He's very anxious that we should...I'm too old...'

'I don't suppose that being in love has anything to do with age,' observed Rosie. 'Of course he wants to marry you; you're still pretty, you know, and you'd make a splendid wife, just the thing for a solicitor. You've spent years looking after Granny, who really doesn't need looking after, especially since there's Elspeth. Is he on the phone?'

Aunt Carrie nodded.

'Good. Ring him up this evening—it's only half-past nine, and tell him you'll marry him, and ask him to come here, and you can tackle Granny together.' She added carefully, 'I don't want to pry, but has he enough money to marry?'

'He's senior partner in an old firm of solicitors; he's quite comfortably off, and he has a lovely house, not big, you know, just right.' Aunt Carrie, having uttered a long sentence without pause, let out a huge sigh.

'Good,' said Rosie, intent on her matchmaking. 'Will you promise to do that? Do it while I'm here if you like.'

'Your grandmother will be angry.' She caught Rosie's eye. 'Very well, dear. I'll phone him and ask him to come tomorrow—when?'

'Tea-time. Granny will have had a rest.' She got up. 'I'm going to bed, Aunt Carrie; I'll leave you to phone—now?'

Sunday was an eventful day. Lying in her bed at the end of it Rosie reviewed its happenings. It had gone smoothly enough until tea-time, when Mr Brodie had arrived. To her relief, Rosie had seen that he was a man of determination. Nothing much to look at, perhaps, but very suitable for Aunt Carrie, and it was obvious that he loved that lady dearly. Over tea and Elspeth's shortbread she had been the unwilling but fascinated witness of his level-headed battle with her grandmother. Mrs Macdonald, taken unawares, and then subjected to the solicitor's dry-as-dust arguments, found herself out-flanked, the ground taken from under her feet and not a leg to stand on. Finally she had conceded that there was no reason why Aunt Carrie shouldn't marry if she wished. Even her caustic 'ridiculous at her age' had conjured up no more than a slight lift of the eyebrows from Aunt Carrie's suitor. He was made of stern stuff, Rosie reflected. She closed her eyes well content with the day's happenings.

It was fortunate that, in the bustle of getting off to the hospital in the morning, her grandmother had little time to grumble about her daughter. Rosie had prudently suggested that her aunt should keep out of sight until they had left, and her grandmother, full of her own affairs, hardly noticed that she wasn't there. Getting the old lady into the taxi took time, and she complained bitterly as it sped through the city, disregarding the cobbled streets away from the main roads. The Royal Infirmary was on the other side of Princes Street, beyond the Grassmarket, towering over the narrow streets and ancient houses around it. Rosie helped her grandmother out of the taxi, went in search of a porter and a wheelchair, and with five minutes to spare presented the pair of them at the X-ray department.

There were any number of people waiting, and she felt uncomfortable as they passed the rows of patients and were ushered at once into the X-ray room. Her grandmother, never particularly mindful of other people's convenience, had taken it for granted that she should be attended to at once, and when the X-ray had been taken expressed the hope that she wouldn't be kept waiting for too long. The radiographer, a brisk man, muttered something, and Rosie wheeled her grandmother away to the waiting-room before the two of them could cross swords.

It was fifteen minutes before a student nurse came to fetch them, wheeling the old lady into a small room, and hurrying away again.

'Why am I brought here?' demanded Mrs Macdonald crossly and, when Rosie pointed out in her calm way that it might be to await the result of the X-ray, told her to hold her tongue until she had something sensible to say. So Rosie stood mute, studying the only picture on the wall, a print of Princes Street. She wished she were there now, browsing round Jenners with plenty of money in her purse.

The door opened and Dr MacLeod came in, followed by Dr Cameron. Rosie felt a surge of pleasure at the sight of him, instantly followed by surprise. Unlike Dr MacLeod he was wearing a long white coat, and looked somehow unapproachable.

He bade her a cheerful good morning, and greeted Mrs Macdonald with brisk kindliness before assuring her that her ankle was very nearly as good as new.

'A stout stick,' he told her, 'and a helping hand from time to time. You have done splendidly.'

Mrs Macdonald had found her voice. 'I was under the impression that you were a general practitioner, helping Dr Finlay.'

Dr Cameron smiled a little, but it was Dr MacLeod who answered her. 'A small misunderstanding,' he said smoothly. 'This is Sir Fergus Cameron, the professor of orthopaedics at this hospital, and senior consultant for the region. You were most fortunate in having his services when you sprained your ankle.'

Rosie blushed with shame when her grandmother said sharply, 'On the National Health, I hope?'

Sir Fergus spoke then, his voice mild. 'Naturally, Mrs Macdonald—indeed, I would gladly waive all fees for the pleasure of making the acquaintance of yourself and your granddaughter.' He stood there, a genial giant, smiling pleasantly, and Rosie wished very much that the ground beneath her feet might open up and swallow her.

He shook hands with her grandmother with the remark

that Dr MacLeod would keep her under his eye for a time, and, with nothing but a murmured goodbye to herself, went away.

Dr MacLeod was inclined to fuss. A porter had to be fetched, a visit arranged, and five minutes was wasted while Mrs Macdonald forecast a gloomy future for herself.

'I am not strong,' she declared. 'My health is probably unimportant to those around me, and I do my utmost to make light of hurtful ailments...'

Her doctor patted her hand. 'You are remarkably fit for a lady of your years,' he assured her, 'and I shall keep my eye upon you.'

Rosie went ahead to get a taxi, hoping for a glimpse of the professor; there was no sign of him. Not that it mattered, she told herself crossly. He had taken not the slightest notice of her, and why should he?

CHAPTER FOUR

ROSIE caught an inter-city train to London the next morning after bidding goodbye first to Aunt Carrie, who in a flurry of half-finished sentences begged her to come to the wedding, 'As soon as it can be arranged. Elspeth knows of a good woman who will come in to help with the house.'

Rosie had kissed her warmly. 'I'll come if I possibly can,' she had said.

Elspeth had hugged her and handed her a packet of sandwiches for the homeward journey. 'It was a joy to have ye, lass. I'll take good care of your granny.'

Lastly, her grandmother, sitting in the drawing-room reading the newspaper had bidden her farewell. Rosie had thanked her for her holiday, which was a bit silly, but she knew it would be expected of her, and her grandmother in her turn offered no thanks for Rosie's care of her. Indeed, she had said dourly, 'You'll miss all the gallivanting with Dr Cameron.'

'Did I gallivant?' asked Rosie with interest, and had to bite back the words on her tongue when her grandmother said,

'And much good it did you, but I dare say it amused him, pretending to be a country doctor.'

Rosie, sitting in her second-class seat, eating her sandwiches and washing them down with British Rail coffee, found that Mrs Macdonald's remark still rankled.

It was lovely to be home. There was a great deal to talk about, not least her unexpected visit to Inverard.

'You see, I didn't know—Dr—not Dr, Professor Cameron, only he's Sir Fergus as well—couldn't stop as it was an emergency call. It hasn't changed, and Mrs MacFee is there still, and old Robert...'

'And no one else? Has he no friend living with him? Surely he is not alone?' asked her father.

'Well, there wasn't anyone there, and as far as I know no one went to see him at the hospital. I went—I had to.'

'Of course you did,' said her mother. 'He'll recover?'

'I don't know. I've got the phone number. The—the professor said it was impossible to tell at the moment.'

'Was he nice, this professor? Scots? How strange that he didn't tell your grandmother who he really was.' Her mother added with a casual air, 'Elderly, I dare say—I mean, being a professor one would expect him to be.'

'Not even elderly, about thirty-five or six, I should think—he's a very big man, and tall. Dark, good-looking. Most of the time we didn't get on together. His own doctor was really rather nice, though—quite young and friendly.'

'I had better telephone the hospital,' said her father. 'And you are sure that your grandmother wishes to have nothing to do with him?'

He came back presently. 'No change. I spoke to Dr Douglas—he asked after you, Rosie.'

'Oh, did he?' She felt her mother's interested eye upon her, and went a little pink. 'He has been looking after Uncle Donald for the last year or two, I believe; he seemed very nice.'

If Mrs Macdonald was disappointed at this wishy-washy statement she didn't say so. 'It is nice to know that your uncle is in competent hands. He's not a consultant?'

'No, no. He has a practice in Oban.'

'Of course, he can call in someone from Edinburgh or Glasgow if he needs a second opinion.'

'Well, yes, only there was no need because Professor Cameron was already there, and he's a consultant.' Rosie frowned. 'Though I don't know what of.'

'Ah, well,' said her mother. 'I dare say we shall hear how your uncle does.'

Sooner than they had expected, as it turned out.

Rosie had been back at her desk, neatly typing Mr Crabbe senior's dry-as-dust letters when Mr Crabbe junior called her on the intercom.

'There is a telephone call for you, Miss Macdonald. As you know, we do not allow private calls in that office, but it seems that this one is urgent. It will be switched through to your office.'

He always referred to the cubby-hole where she worked as an office.

She thanked him while half a dozen dire possibilities left her with a dry mouth. She lifted the receiver, and Professor Cameron's voice said, 'Ah, good morning, Rosie.'

'It's you!' she exclaimed. 'I thought something awful had happened at home.' She let out the breath she had been holding. 'How did you know that I was here? Is Grandmother ill? But you wouldn't know that, would you? Dr MacLeod would have phoned——'

'Stop nattering. I'm a busy man, and presumably you're doing whatever it is you do. Your uncle died early this morning.'

'Oh—oh, I'm sorry. I didn't like him, but all the same I'm sorry.'

'He had been unconscious for several hours. His solicitor and Dr Douglas will be in touch with your father. Goodbye, Rosie.'

He had rung off before she could thank him.

When she got home that evening her father told her that he had had a telephone call from Dr Douglas. 'It seems that there is no one on his side of the family— only those in Canada. I shall have to go to the funeral. They will let me know when it is to be. I'll go up by train, and stay with your grandmother.'

There was a letter from the solicitor in the morning, too, suggesting that Mr Macdonald might wish to attend the funeral on what was now the following day, so Rosie drove her father to the station and saw him off, and then went back to the office to spend the morning in the dimly lighted basement looking for documents for old Mr Crabbe while she wondered if by any chance her father might meet Professor Cameron. She pulled out a bundle of old papers covered in dust, and sneezed. It was most unlikely.

Her father telephoned that evening, merely to say that he had arrived safely, and was at her grandmother's house. The funeral was the next day, and Aunt Carrie and her fiancé were going to drive him to Oban.

'Your granny isn't going to like that,' observed her mother as she put the phone down. 'I'm so very glad that Carrie is going to get married.'

She started down the flagstone passage to the kitchen.
'I'll start the supper, love, if you'll lay the table. Your
father will be back in two days' time—the house is empty
without him, isn't it?'

Her father phoned again the following evening to tell
them that he would be home the next day.

'He sounded tired,' observed his wife, who had taken
the call. 'Well, I suppose it was tiredness—as though
something had happened...'

'I dare say he is tired,' said Rosie comfortingly. 'It's
quite a journey to Edinburgh, and then driving to Oban
and back today. I hope he'll rest on Sunday before he
goes back to work. Did he say what time he would get
here?'

'No—and I quite forgot to ask him. We'll have a casserole, then it won't matter, will it? Will you be able to
get home a bit earlier?'

Rosie said yes, of course, Mr Twitchett had kept her
during her lunch-hour that day; she would point that
out to him in the morning, and leave as soon after her
lunch-break as she could.

Mr Twitchett wasn't best pleased, but he was forced
to admit that she had missed half an hour of her lunch
hour, and since it was an urgent family matter he had
no choice but to allow her to go home during the early
afternoon. There had been no message from her father,
she and her mother had tea, put the casserole in the oven,
and Rosie occupied herself in making a treacle tart.

A rather watery sun shone into the kitchen, touching
lightly on Hobb, her father's labrador, who had come
with them from Inverard, and now that he was elderly
led a leisurely life, sleeping a great deal and keeping the
family cat company before the Aga. The sun also rested

on Rosie as she stood at the kitchen table making her pastry, and it showed up the worn paintwork and shabby chairs. All the same, the kitchen was a pleasant room with bright curtains and the vase of early roses she had picked from the New Dawn climber outside the front door. Mrs Macdonald switched on the radio for the six o'clock news, and neither of them heard the car stop outside the house.

It was Rosie who heard the rumble of voices first.

'That's Father!' she cried. 'And there's someone with him.' Her mother had got up to open the door just as her father came in, and, right behind him, Sir Fergus Cameron.

Rosie, the tart on its plate held in one hand while she neatened its edge with a knife, put them both down carefully, very conscious of her pinny and floury hands. She looked vaguely at her father embracing her mother, and allowed her astonished gaze to dwell on Professor Cameron. After a moment she said 'Hello' in an enquiring voice.

By then her father was introducing him to her mother, and it was a few moments before the guest said, 'Hello, Rosie! I had to come this way—it was pleasant to have your father's company.'

'You're a long way from home,' she commented, and blushed at the silliness of the remark.

'Home is where the heart is,' he told her gravely, and turned to make a civil answer to her mother's offer of a bed for the night.

'I'm expected at Bristol,' he told her.

'Then at least do stay for supper,' urged Mrs Macdonald. 'A casserole, and Rosie has made a treacle tart. You must be hungry?'

He smiled. 'I am, and I would be delighted to have supper with you.'

Mrs Macdonald beamed at him. 'Oh, splendid. Go along the pair of you, and have a drink while we get it on the table.'

When they had gone she said, 'Put that tart in the oven, love, it should be just about ready to eat by the time they've had a drink and we've had the casserole. What a nice young man.'

Rosie put the tart in the oven and said nothing. Sir Fergus was indeed a long way from home, and what on earth had he meant about home being where the heart was? His home was in Scotland. She took off her pinny, and went away to tidy herself, and presently joined the others in the pleasant, rather shabby sitting-room.

Her father gave her a glass of sherry and, her mother observed, 'It's a long drive from Edinburgh...'

It was really a question.

'We left early this morning, there wasn't much traffic, and I enjoy driving.' Sir Fergus didn't sound in the least tired, and he didn't look it, either. He looked perfectly at home, thought Rosie, peeping at him when he wasn't looking.

'I am most grateful,' said her father quietly. 'It was a pleasant journey, and far less tiresome than that long train ride. I had a great deal to think about, and the time to do it.' He looked at his wife. 'I have a great deal to tell you, my dear...'

'I'll go and see to the supper,' offered Rosie, and very much to her surprise Sir Fergus got up too.

'I'm sure there is something I can do to help you,' he said smoothly, and her father said,

'Oh, Fergus, be so good as to tell Rosie my news while you're dishing up—you will excuse us if we have just a few minutes to talk?'

So it's Fergus, is it? thought Rosie, leading the way to the kitchen. And what is this news?

She said, 'Sit down, do. We're going to eat here because it's warm, and we weren't expecting guests...' She turned swiftly. 'I'm sorry, that sounded rude, but I didn't mean it to be. Only perhaps you don't eat in the kitchen, being a professor; if we had known that you were coming we would have used the dining-room.'

'I like kitchens.' He sat down on the edge of the table. 'Something smells delicious.'

'Beef casserole, dumplings and mashed potatoes.' She took the saucepan off the sink, drained it, and began to beat the contents with a fork.

'Quite the little housewife,' murmured the professor.

'Well, not so little.'

Rosie added a generous knob of butter, and went on beating, looking annoyed.

'That doesn't mean to say you're large,' he went on equably. 'In fact, you appear to me to be just right...'

She shot in some milk and plied her fork. 'Stop annoying me, Sir Fergus. What news?'

'Your uncle has left Inverard to your father. He left a good deal of money besides. Most of it goes to distant relations in Canada, but there is sufficient for your father to run the place and return to sheep-farming.'

She had abandoned the potatoes. 'Is that really true?' And then, at the look on his face, added, 'Oh, sorry, no one ever doubts your word; it's just that I'm a bit overcome.'

'Naturally. It may interest you to know that your uncle altered his will after he had seen you.'

She echoed him in a bemused fashion. 'Seen me? After he had seen me?'

'You sound like a parrot. There is a delicious smell of toasted treacle.'

'My tart!' Rosie flung open the Aga oven door, snatched out the tart, and put it on the table. It was exactly right, the pastry pale brown and flaky and the treacle bubbling. The fragrance of it caused Sir Fergus's patrician nose to flare with pleasure.

He asked, 'Are you glad?'

'Glad? I'm dumbfounded—over the moon. Wouldn't you be, in my shoes?'

'Indeed I would. You will no longer need to pound a typewriter, will you? But you must have some friends here whom you will miss?'

He was watching her, sleepy-eyed.

'Well, of course I have some friends; we have been here for six years. There's Brenda up at the big house; we play tennis and go shopping and that kind of thing, and there's Will—we go fishing sometimes...'

'Will?' prompted the professor gently.

'He's a nice boy, waiting to go up to Oxford...'

'So you have no regrets at leaving?' He spoke casually.

'None—oh, I've been happy here, but I long to be back at Inverard.'

She smiled widely at him. 'I can't quite believe it, you know.' She put the saucepan with the potatoes in it back on the Aga to keep warm, and asked, 'Are you very hungry?' She added, 'There's such a lot of you, isn't there?'

'Er—yes, I'm afraid so.'

Mrs Macdonald came into the kitchen followed by her husband, and the professor got up from the table, saying easily, 'It is really very good of you, Mrs Macdonald, to invite me to supper.'

'A small return for bringing my husband home, Sir Fergus!'

She beamed at him, and Rosie said quietly to her father, 'I'm still trying to believe it's true, Father. Can we go soon?'

'Just as soon as there is someone to take over from me, my darling. Fergus, you'll have a glass of beer with your supper? Something smells good.'

Supper was a cheerful meal, the talk naturally enough centred round Scotland—the Highlands and Inverard in particular—and Rosie was surprised to discover that Sir Fergus, without pushing himself forward in any way, became, as it were, integrated into the conversation. It seemed that he knew several old friends of her parents, had an excellent knowledge of the country round Oban and Fort William, and at the same time betrayed a sound knowledge of Edinburgh.

And yet, she thought uneasily, he had told them nothing about himself. That he had some kind of consultant position at the Royal Infirmary seemed obvious, on the other hand he seemed to have a good deal of free time. He had been on holiday, hadn't he, when they had met? And now he had said that he was going to Bristol. For how long? she wondered. He had told her that he hoped to marry; perhaps the girl lived there. She wondered where they had met; Bristol and Edinburgh were very far apart...

'Rosie, dear.'

Her mother's voice broke into her thoughts.

'Will you help me take the coffee into the sitting-room?'

And Rosie looked up to find the professor's eyes on her.

He looked amused, and she flushed a little, aware that she had allowed her thoughts to stray—about him, too.

She became all at once very brisk, serving the coffee, and carrying on a laboured conversation with the professor, who, for his part, replied to her stilted comments with suitable gravity and enjoyed himself enormously.

He got up to go presently, assuring them that he hoped they might meet again when they returned to their home in Scotland. 'You can reach me at the Royal Infirmary,' he told them, 'and perhaps I shall be able to return your hospitality, Mrs Macdonald?'

'Oh, I do hope so.' Mrs Macdonald tiptoed to kiss his cheek, and said, 'You were so kind to my mother-in-law, and I'm sure Rosie was delighted to have some young company.'

'I'm flattered,' he murmured, and held out a hand to Rosie, who shook it with her eyes fixed on his tie, and mumbled awkwardly.

Bother the man, she thought. Making me feel a fool!

After he had gone they sat up until late discussing a suddenly delightful future. They wouldn't be able to go at once, of course; her father reckoned that it would be at least a month before he could leave his job. There would be the furniture to sell, for they had taken only their personal possessions when they had left Inverard, but the house went with his job, which would simplify their move.

'It is early days for planning, but perhaps it would be a good idea if your mother and I took Hobb and

Simpkins, the china and glass and so forth and as many clothes as we can pack in, and you, Rosie, go by train with the rest of the luggage. Could you manage that?'

'Yes, of course. You'll leave a day ahead of me—you'll have to spend a night on the way. Will you go to Granny's first?'

'I think not—we can cross over at Carlisle, and go straight up from there. Could you manage to change trains at Waverley Station? I could meet you at Crianlarich.'

'I can't wait!' declared Mrs Macdonald happily. 'Did you say everything looks the same, dear?'

'As far as I could see. Mrs MacFee and Old Robert certainly haven't changed.'

'To meet old friends again...' She sighed with pleasure. 'Of course, we shall have to have this Dr Douglas now he's taken over the practice. He sounds very nice.' She looked at Rosie. 'You'll have a chance to meet some young people, darling.'

Which remark Rosie rightly translated as having a chance to see more of Dr Douglas, single and most suitable. He was, as her mother had said, a nice man, which made it all the more strange that Sir Fergus's austere visage should superimpose itself upon the younger man's pleasant features.

On Monday she begged an interview with old Mr Crabbe, and gave him her notice. He was no more than a figure-head in the firm now; his son and young Mr Twitchett conducted the business with the aid of computers, word processors and every modern gadget which might enable them to take on more work. He sat in his backwater of an office, surrounded by deed boxes and stacks of papers and shelves of law books, and Rosie, who liked him, felt sorry to be leaving him, although she was glad enough to turn her back on her typewriter. She thought happily of Inverard and the life she would lead there. She would take over the kitchen garden once more, and the hens, and help Flora around the house, and there would be time to knit; she was a skilled knitter, and like many girls and women in the Highlands had spent the long winter evenings making the traditional sweaters. She had had no trouble in selling them to shops in Fort William and Oban, and they were always in demand, especially by tourists.

It had seemed to her at first that the month before they could return to her old home would be far too long, but the days were filled with packing, giving farewell dinners to the friends they had made and, once she had left her job, the task of helping her father hand over the considerable bookwork to his successor.

The last day came, and she saw her mother and father off early in the morning with Hobb and Simpkins cocooned in the most precious of the family possessions, and the boot stuffed to capacity. She waved until they were out of sight, and then went into the house. She wouldn't be leaving until the next day, and there was a good deal to do before then. The house must be left clean and tidy for the new tenants, and there were the last of the cases to finish packing. Two big trunks had been sent on in advance, but there were always last-minute things which she would have to take with her. The day went quickly, she had no time to be lonely; she cooked supper and went to bed early, and was up at first light to eat a hasty breakfast, cast an eye over the house for the last time, and then get into the taxi to take her to the station.

It was a two-hour train journey to London, but once there she found that the queue for taxis was long and slow-moving; she missed the train to Edinburgh she had planned to catch, and sat impatiently, drinking coffee she didn't want, until she could board the next train, see to her cases, and settle into a corner seat for the journey north. She was excited now, still not quite believing that she was going back to her old life once more, but she was tired too, and dozed off, only to wake and find that they had reached Berwick-on-Tweed, and Edinburgh was no longer a dream but a reality barely forty minutes or so away.

Waverley Station was busy and bright with the late-afternoon sunshine. Rosie collected her hand-luggage and got out of the coach, intent on getting the luggage and then telephoning her father to say that she would be on a later train to Crianlarich.

She had one foot on the platform when she had her overnight bag taken from her and Sir Fergus said,

'Hello, Rosie. Where's the rest of the luggage?'

She gaped at him. 'How did you know...? I missed the train at King's Cross... Are you going somewhere?'

'Plenty of time to talk later,' he told her easily. 'Is the luggage in the front van?'

She nodded, and stood watching his commanding figure stride away, her surprise at last giving way to good sense. She hurried after him, and plucked at his sleeve. 'I'm catching the next train—there's one to Fort William in half an hour...'

'I'm going to Fort William with the car; I'll drop you off.' He picked up the luggage. 'The car's outside; come along.'

Since he had the luggage she went. When they reached the car she tried again. 'Look, it's out of your way—and how did you know?'

'Your father told me. Get in, there's a good girl.' Rosie eyed the car. 'It's the Rolls-Royce again.' She turned an accusing eye upon him. 'It's yours, isn't it? You were pretending . . .'

'I had no need. I wasn't asked, if you remember.' He was stowing the luggage in the boot. 'Are you coming or not?'

Put like that there was nothing much she could do about it. She got in and settled thankfully into the comfort of the big car.

He got in beside her, and as he drove off asked, 'Tired?'

She thought back over a long day. 'Yes.'

'When did you last have a meal? And I don't mean a sandwich on the train.'

Thinking about it, she realised that she hadn't; breakfast had been a slice of toast and a pot of tea, and then a sandwich at King's Cross, and then a cardboard mug of tea on the train and two rich tea biscuits in plastic.

'Well, at supper, last night.'

He growled something at her, but she wasn't listening. She was suddenly sleepy; for the first time that day she had no worries. Here she was, borne in luxury, the luggage safely stowed, and home only an hour or two away. She closed her eyes and went to sleep.

He woke her very gently as he drew up before the Inverbeg Inn at the upper end of Loch Lomond. She opened her eyes, and sat up at once. 'Oh, Luss already; I went to sleep.'

'Now I hope you are as hungry as I am?' He leant over and undid her seatbelt, and then got out to open her door.

She hung back. 'But I'm sure there'll be a meal for me when I get home—don't stop on my account.'

'I'm stopping on both our accounts.'

He whisked her into the inn without more ado, sat her down at the bar, watched her drink her sherry, and then said, 'Go and tidy your face or whatever while I see what there is to eat. I'll be here.'

So she went away and did her face and her hair, feeling a bit strange because of the sherry on an empty stomach, and then she went back to join him. He handed her the menu and offered her another sherry.

'No, thank you, I feel rather peculiar as it is. May I have the poached salmon?'

He said gravely, 'You may; and I would suggest that you try the mushrooms in garlic butter to start with. A cucumber salad with the fish, or would you rather have spinach?'

'Oh, the cucumber, please.'

The dining-room was half full and pleasant; they ate their meal without haste, exchanging small talk of an undemanding nature, and presently got back into the Rolls and drove on. There were rather less then forty miles to go, and since the road for most of the way was a good one, and the Rolls swallowed the miles with well-bred speed, Rosie calculated that she would be home well within the hour. Her pleasure at the thought was tinged with regret that Sir Fergus would bid her a polite goodbye and very likely never see her again. Not that she minded that, she reminded herself stoutly, only if

she could get to know him better she might be able to
discover why she still wasn't sure if she liked him or not.

'Now you are home again what do you intend to do?'
asked her companion suddenly.

'Help Mother run the house, help old Robert with the
garden, I don't know if Uncle Donald kept chickens,
but I shall, and in the winter I shall knit. We had a kind
of cottage industry, you know, and sold what we had
knitted to the shops in Oban and Fort William.'

'Will you be content with that?'

She said, suddenly fierce. 'Have you ever sat at a desk
from nine till five typing letters full of long words and
dry as dust?' She cast a look at his profile, and saw that
he was smiling. 'Oh, of course you haven't,' she went
on crossly. 'If you had, you would know that anything
is better than that.'

'Better than marrying?'

'Well, of course not. That is, if one married the right
person—there can't be anything better than that.'

He said idly, 'You're a very pretty girl; one would
assume that you have had your chances.'

'Oh, yes. Perhaps I'm hard to please.'

'Perhaps you have never fallen in love and loved too?'

'Have you?'

'Oh, yes. It brings its difficulties, but they will be
overcome in due course.'

They drove in silence for a while until he said, 'Here's
your turning,' and slid the Rolls on to the narrow country
lane she knew so well.

The daylight was beginning to fade very slowly, its
pearly light enhancing the colours around them, so that
the mountains, never far away, showed steely grey, and

the firs crowding their lower reaches had become a vivid green in the evening light.

'I can't believe it,' murmured Rosie softly. 'It doesn't change, does it?'

He understood her. 'No, but the best time of day is early in the morning.'

'Oh, yes, about six o'clock. I don't suppose you get much chance to enjoy that, though. Do you come to stay with Dr Finlay very often?'

'Not as often as I would wish. Do you fish, Rosie?'

'Yes. There's splendid trout fishing here you know; salmon, too.'

They were almost in sight of the house now, and Rosie sat forward so that she would get the first delightful glimpse. There were lights in most of the windows downstairs, and as they swept gently up to the front door it was thrown open and her mother and father, Hobb and Simpkins with Mrs MacFee and Old Robert behind them came out to meet them.

Rosie was hugged and kissed as though she hadn't been seen for years, while Hobb and Simpkins wound themselves around her legs, and it was her father who held out a hand to Sir Fergus and said, 'We are so grateful to you. Do come in and have coffee and a sandwich . . .'

'And stay the night,' added Mrs Macdonald quickly. 'We have rooms enough now, and we would love to have you.' She cast a motherly eye over him. 'You're tired—could you not stay?'

Rosie had turned to look at him. 'It would be nice if you could; you've been so kind, and I haven't thanked you properly.'

He gave a wicked little grin and looked at her from under drooping lids, and she found herself, to her great annoyance, going red.

It was to her mother, however, that he spoke. 'It would be delightful, but I am expected tonight.'

'Then you'll have a cup of coffee?'

He said regretfully, 'Not even a cup of coffee, Mrs Macdonald, but I hope that if I come this way in the future you will invite me again.'

To Rosie's astonishment her mother stood on tiptoe and kissed his cheek, and that was the second time.

'I do hope that someone looks after you properly. We won't keep you.'

He shook Mr Macdonald's hand, bade Mrs MacFee and Old Robert goodbye, and turned to Rosie. She broke into speech before he could utter a word.

'Thank you for bringing me, and for my dinner—you've been very kind.' She was conscious that she had said it all before more than once, and she felt a fool under his cool look.

'A pleasure, Rosie, goodbye.'

He got into the car and drove himself back up the lane, and they all stood and watched until he was out of sight.

'Such a nice man,' observed her mother, 'don't you think so Rosie?'

Rosie said, 'Yes, Mother,' quite unable to voice her muddled thoughts; of course he was nice. He was also a man who liked his own way and expected to get it; moreover she knew nothing about him. Did he live in Edinburgh? she wondered. And why was he going to Fort William? Was that where the girl he was going to marry lived? And if so, why couldn't he have said so?

They all went indoors, and the rest of the evening was taken up with the exchange of news.

She pottered around getting ready for bed. She was back in her own room once again, and it was as though she had never left it. Uncle Donald had made very few alterations in the house, and the furniture was almost exactly as she remembered it. At length she had a bath in the rather old-fashioned bathroom at her end of the house and, since it was a lovely night, went to hang out of the window. It was a clear night and starry, a small wind stirred the trees around the house, which somehow added to the peace. Rosie allowed her thoughts to roam in a sleepy fashion. Only they didn't roam far; they stopped at Sir Fergus.

'I'm not really interested in him,' she said out loud, her wits woolly with sleep. 'But it would be nice to know more about him.'

She got into bed, and Simpkins, who was already there, opened an eye and looked annoyed at being disturbed.

'I wonder what sort of a girl she is?' Rosie asked of the little cat and, since there was no answer, put her head on the pillow and went to sleep.

CHAPTER FIVE

SIR FERGUS CAMERON drove back the way he had come, but when he reached the road again he turned the car in the direction of Fort William. There was almost no traffic, only a stray sheep from time to time and an occasional small hotel or youth hostel by the side of the road, for it was used during the summer months by a great many walkers. At Fort William he turned off to Banavie and so to Glenfinnan; this was Cameron country now, and he was almost home.

Through Glenfinnan and very shortly a glimpse of Loch Eilt and then the two gate-posts, the gates opening on to a narrow drive winding between trees beside the water. He rounded a corner and saw his family home ahead. A magnificent house—a sixteenth-century fortified house, added to, modernised, but very little altered over the years. It had square towers at each end of it, and corbelled battlements, long, wide windows on the lower floors, and very small dormer ones tucked into irregular roofs. The stout door was set at an angle between the front of the house and a short wing at right angles to it.

As he drew up the door was opened by an old man, tall and very thin with a rugged face and an eye-patch. Sir Fergus got out of the car, and crossed to him in two strides.

'Good evening, Hamish. I'm late. Is my mother still up?'

'Aye, Sir Fergus, and disappointed that it is too late for a guid blether!' He took the professor's bag from him. 'Ye'll be biding a wee while?'

'Until tomorrow evening. How's the rheumatism?'

The old man hesitated, 'Weel...'

Sir Fergus put a gentle hand on the man's shoulder. 'I'll have a look at you before I go.'

He crossed the hall, large and square with its flag-stoned floor partly covered by a beautiful worn carpet, its low curved ceiling and plain plastered walls, he opened a door to one side of the oak staircase, and entered a charming sitting-room. It had a plaster-work ceiling, rather crude strap-work—several hundred years old— and a Saxe blue wallpaper of a much later date. The furniture was a pleasing mixture of cretonne-covered chairs and several small tables, a Louis XV writing table under the one long and narrow window, and a bombe commode. There were a great many small pictures on the walls and a small ormolu Cartel clock on the narrow mantelshelf.

His mother was in one of the chairs, knitting, but she got up as he crossed the room—a woman in her sixties, rather stout, grey hair framing serene good looks.

She put up her face for his kiss. 'My dear, you must be tired; Hamish will bring you coffee and sandwiches. Such a pity that you have to go again so soon. Your secretary said that you were due in Leiden for a con-sultation, but lovely to see you, and so unexpected.'

He had taken a chair opposite her, and the Jack Russell who had been sitting with her went to sit with him and put his chin on the professor's shoes. He smiled a little at his mother's remark, for it had sounded like a question.

'I'm late because I gave someone a lift. You remember me telling you about the Macdonalds at Inverard?'

'Oh, yes—he died, did he not? Donald Macdonald. You were called to old Mrs Macdonald at Bridge of Orchy—there was a granddaughter...'

'Rosie, and a more inappropriate name would be hard to find.' He had bent down to pull gently at the Jack Russell's ears and didn't see her quick look. 'Malcolm Macdonald, her father who lived there originally, has inherited, and they've moved back there. I collected Rosie and some luggage from Waverley Station this evening, and drove her up. Her parents had already come up by car.'

'How kind, dear, especially if I remember rightly you said you neither of you have much time to waste on each other.'

He laughed. 'That's true; we have to try hard to be civil, but we seem to have a mutual antipathy.'

He began to talk about family matters then, and Hamish came in with the coffee and sandwiches, and his mother, placidly knitting and making appropriate replies to his remarks, wondered about Rosie.

Fergus, she reflected, was thirty-five, and although he had fancied himself in love on a number of occasions she was sure that he had never been serious; none of the girls had been suitable, she considered. He needed a wife to stand up to him; he was a successful man, self-assured, well-to-do, and inclined to be impatient and like his own way—things which he concealed very well under beautiful manners and, when he troubled to exert himself, great charm. This Rosie sounded exactly right...

They sat talking for an hour or so before she got up to go to bed. 'Any plans for tomorrow?' she wanted to know as she bade him goodnight.

'An hour's fishing before breakfast. A pity I didn't bring Gyp with me, but I wasn't sure how much luggage Rosie would have.'

'You'll manage a few days before the summer's over? She can come then.'

He went to open the door for her,

'Bobby will stay down here with you—let him into my room as you come up, will you, dear?'

The professor went back to his chair, pouring himself a nightcap as he went. He was tired, but it was pleasant to sit in the peaceful room with Bobby at his feet. He allowed his thoughts to wander, and presently found himself wishing that Rosie was sitting with him. 'A tiresome girl,' he observed to the little dog, 'but her conversation is stimulating, to say the least—that is if we aren't arguing!' He sighed. 'She'll make young Douglas a good wife.'

He went through the quiet old house presently, using the secondary staircase leading from an inner corridor in the main part of the house. His room overlooked the grounds at the back of his home; he spent ten minutes there with Bobby, and stood listening to the wind in the trees and the soft lapping of the water at the loch's edge, and once again he wished that Rosie were with him. He laughed at himself, and went back into the house.

As for Rosie, she hadn't given him a thought, there was so much to talk about and, in the morning, so much to do. After all, Mrs MacFee and Old Robert had six years' events to tell about, and there was furniture to rearrange, odds and ends which had been banished to the attics to be brought down into the house once more, and a detailed tour of the gardens to be made. Uncle Donald hadn't bothered much with flowers; the kitchen garden flourished—there was enough stuff there to keep Rosie and her mother busy bottling and freezing for days—but the rose garden and the herbaceous borders had been neglected. Rosie went round pulling up weeds and frowning over roses which hadn't been cut back for years while Old Robert stumped along beside her explaining that Donald Macdonald wouldn't allow him so much as a boy to give a hand, and forbade him to waste his time on flowers.

'Never mind, Robert. I shall enjoy getting everything going again. The kitchen garden looks pretty good to me; you must have worked very hard.'

'Oh, aye,' said Old Robert.

It was that afternoon, after her father had come in from a leisurely inspection of the land around the house, and she was crossing the inner hall with a vase of flowers she had wrested from the weedy beds, that he stopped to say,

'Rosie, come to the study, will you? There's something I would like you to do for me.'

She put the flowers in the drawing-room, and opened the door leading from it, and went into a long, low room with a big window overlooking the gardens at the side of the house—a room lined with books, and furnished as it had been for years, with bulky leather armchairs, a great desk and a circular table in its centre.

'I've had a letter from your granny. She wants to come and see us.' Her father picked up the letter on his desk. 'She says that she wishes to see the house and us before she dies; she also says that someone will have to fetch her here. Carrie, it seems, is no longer of any use to her, and she asks that you should go and fetch her here and drive her back to Edinburgh at the end of her visit.'

He saw the look on Rosie's face, and said, 'Yes, I know, dear, but she has always loved this place. After all, she came here as a bride . . . I wondered if you would like to go and stay for a day or two before you pick her up . . . You've had a thin time of it for the last few years, and now I'm going to give you a cheque to spend on clothes—you should be able to fit yourself out in Edinburgh. I had a chat with Dr MacLeod, and he kindly suggested that you should stay with him and his wife for a night or two. Granny need not know, and you can shop to your heart's content.'

He handed her a cheque, and watched her lovely face break into a wide smile. 'Father—but this is much too much . . . I can manage with far less.'

'You don't need to. And it is not too much. If you care to do a little simple arithmetic you will find that I have given you exactly half of the total amount of money you gave your mother while you were working.'

'Yes, but I didn't mind.'

'We know that, my dear. Now we would like you to spend this money on yourself. I dare say you'll pick up old friends again, and you'll need clothes.'

She gave him a hug and waltzed off, her head already full of plans. Most of the clothes would have to be sensible; social life was restricted, especially in the winter, but one or two pretty dresses for dinner parties would be a must—a good suit, too. There was plenty of wear in her old kilt still, but a cashmere sweater would liven it up a bit. Shoes and a pair of fashionable boots as well as the tough wellies she used so often in the winter. A waxed jacket, a blouse or two, and wool so that she could start knitting...

She went back into the garden and did some more weeding while she spent the cheque in a dozen different ways.

There was an elderly Rover in the garage which her uncle had used when he had been living at Inverard, a suitable vehicle in which to convey old Mrs Macdonald from Edinburgh, and Rosie, the cheque cashed in Oban, wearing the best of her last year's summer dresses—an unassuming pale green cotton jersey—flung an over-night-bag into the back of the Rover, and set off for Edinburgh.

It was a splendid morning, the mountains gleamed in the sun, and in the glens the rivers tumbled along over great boulders. Rosie bowled along, not going fast for there was too much to see; there was a need to refresh her memory, and there was time enough. When she reached Bridge of Orchy she stopped on an impulse and went into the hotel and had coffee, exchanging news with the owner. It was surprising that news travelled so fast in that sparsely populated part of Scotland; he knew all about her uncle's death and the return of her mother and father to Inverard. 'Delighted we are, too, Miss Macdonald. We hope we shall see something of you.'

She replied suitably, got back into the car, and drove on, taking the road which Sir Fergus had taken, which, naturally enough, reminded her of him.

Edinburgh is a large place, she reminded herself once more; I'm not at all likely to see anything of him.

Doctor MacLeod and his wife welcomed her warmly, gave her high tea, and showed her into a pretty bedroom.

'You do just as you like,' said Mrs MacLeod. 'You have all tomorrow in which to shop, so come and go just as you please.'

Sound advice which Rosie took. She was out early the next day, in and out of the Princes Street shops, ending up, as she knew she would, in Jenners. She emerged hours later with a great many parcels which necessitated her hailing a taxi to take her back to Doctor MacLeod's house, and once there, since there was no one at home save the daily maid, she repaired to her room and spent the next hour trying on the things she had bought. She had spent almost every penny her father had given her on a couple of pretty summer dresses, a sensible raincoat, cotton skirts and tops and, with an eye on the autumn, a good tweed suit in tawny browns, and also since she had money to burn, an elegant dress for the evening. It was chiffon and taffeta in old rose, with a wide skirt and a wide neckline. It wasn't a very suitable dress perhaps, and she had bought it for a reason which she refused to admit, even to herself. It would be nice, she had reflected, looking at her enticing figure in the looking-glass in Jenners' gown department, if the next time she met the professor she could be wearing it.

It had been silly to buy it, she admitted to herself, trying it on once more, and then hanging it away at the back of the wardrobe at Mrs MacLeod's house. She then turned her attention to the lace undies and slippers and all the small luxuries she had done without during the past six years; it had been such fun shopping for pleasure and not from necessity.

She stowed her purchases in the car the following morning and, after bidding the MacLeods goodbye, drove to her grandmother's house.

That lady, recovered now from her sprained ankle, was none the less full of small complaints. Her own daughter, she declared in a dignified moan, could no longer be bothered with her, and why a woman of her age should wish to marry when she had a perfectly good home of her own was something not to be understood. Rosie murmured from time to time, and exchanged speaking glances with her aunt, who, as far as she could see, had become a different woman. Love wrought miracles, presumably.

'I shall stay with you for one week,' said her grandmother, 'and it is to be hoped that I shall be driven back in comfort. I am an old lady——' she fixed Rosie with a stern eye '—unlike you younger, thoughtless young women, I consider my health before everything else.'

Rosie sternly suppressed a naughty reply, and said, 'Yes, Granny, I'll bring you back in a week's time.'

'Since your aunt Carrie has seen fit to go away and not return until two days after I get back here I shall expect you to stay, Rosie.'

Rosie, trying to think of a good excuse, caught her Aunt's eye, and said 'Yes, Granny' in a meek way instead. Aunt Carrie deserved some fun even though she was middle-aged.

Rosie was loading the car boot with the impedimenta considered necessary for a week's stay by her grandmother when she straightened up to see Sir Fergus driving past in the Rolls. He didn't stop; probably he hadn't seen her, and even if he had she doubted if he would have bothered to do so.

She poked in her grandmother's spare walking stick, her sunshade, her umbrella and a particular cushion she simply *had* to have with her, and then she slammed down the boot with unwonted vigour...

He could have stopped, she grumbled silently, and he must have seen her... Even if it had only been for a moment to make some caustic remark. A slight sound made her turn her head. The Rolls was within inches of her, and Sir Fergus was getting out.

It was annoying to blush so hotly, and his faintly amused look didn't help. She said, 'Good morning, Sir Fergus,' in a rather high voice.

'Hello, Rosie. How fortunate that I should have noticed the car.'

Not her she reflected crossly, the car.

'Are you going back to Inverard?'

She said 'Yes' rather ungraciously and, since he was waiting for her to say something else, added, 'Granny is to pay us a visit, so I came down to get her.'

'Rather unwillingly, perhaps? You were ramming the boot full in a rage.'

'Well...there's such a lot to do and see, and for a week I won't be able to do any of the things I want to do. And now call me selfish...'

Her dark eyes flashed and she had gone rather pink again. The professor, leaning on the bonnet of his car, observed her splendid bosom heaving with temper and longing with suitable appreciation.

'Of course you're not selfish.' He spoke in a soothing manner which took the wind out of her angry sails. 'I can imagine how you feel—you need a week tramping around the hills, don't you? Catching up on memories?

When she nodded he continued, 'Well, now, if you could bear with me we could spend a day together next week? I have to go to Oban, Fort William and then

Inverness, and I've a couple of days owing to me.' He
eyed her narrowly, watching the doubt in her face. 'I
suggest this merely because, while it would be difficult
for you to go off on your own, if I invite you I think
your grandmother would be unable to raise any objection. Presumably she is expecting you to keep her
company for a good deal of the time?'

'Yes, yes, she is. Father will be busy with solicitors,
then Mother has the house to run.'

'Perhaps for one day you could arrange something?'

'It's kind of you.'

'Yes, I know—I'm a kind man, only you don't know
me well enough to realise that.'

She wasn't sure if he was serious; there was nothing
in his face to give her a hint. 'Well, I dare say Granny
might like a quiet day...'

'Splendid. I'll give you a ring if I may. Do you like
walking in the rain?'

'Yes. Anyway, it rains a great deal in the Highlands.'

He looked amused for a moment. 'Yes. Well, I must
be getting on—I've an out patients clinic to keep me
busy this afternoon.' He bent forward and ran a gentle
finger down her cheek. 'You're quite eye-catching when
you're in a rage, but when you're happy you are beautiful.' At her round eyed-astonishment he added, 'And
how's that for coals of fire? Goodbye, Rosie!'

He got into his car and drove off, leaving her with her
pretty mouth slightly open, and for once at a loss for
words; even her thoughts didn't make sense.

She went back into the house to be dragged into the
dining-room by Aunt Carrie. 'Rosie, you're a darling to
stay a day or two when you bring your grandmother
back. You see, we plan to buy some furniture and things,

you know, and go to the theatre, and I thought if—and we want to see about getting married. It's such a...'

Aunt Carrie paused, looking wistful.

'That's fine,' said Rosie, who hadn't been listening, 'I'll stay two days when we get back—will that be long enough?' As she spoke she wondered if she might see the professor then. Of course, if they spent a day walking together they probably wouldn't be on speaking terms.

They could hear her grandmother's voice raised in protest about something or other, and Rosie kissed her aunt's cheek and nipped into the hall.

'There you are. I am quite ready, and I expect you to be as well, Rosie. Let us get into the car.'

Rosie had plenty of time to think as they drove back, too, for her grandmother kept up a running monologue—a mixture of fault-finding, directed at Aunt Carrie, Elspeth, tradespeople and those of her friends who had annoyed her in some way, interlarded with a detailed account of her numerous ailments. Rosie, murmuring suitably from time to time, thought about Sir Fergus and admired the scenery. She knew it very well, but there was always something new to see. A day out would be lovely; it would probably be raining, but who cared? Rannoch Moor, she thought with longing, its countless pools sparkling under the rain-clouds.

'You are not listening, Rosie,' said her grandmother. 'We seem to have been in this car for a very long time.'

'Not long now, Granny. Here's Bridge of Orchy—remember the hotel? Mother will be waiting for us with tea. Almost nothing has changed—the drawing-room is exactly the same as it always was.'

She was surprised when old Mrs Macdonald commented, 'It will be pleasant to talk to your mother again.'

The old lady's welcome was all that she could have wished for; her son and daughter-in-law were at the door to receive her, with Mrs MacFee hovering in the background ready to take the baggage Rosie was hurling out of the boot. Installed in a comfortable chair in the drawing-room, old Mrs Macdonald pronounced herself well pleased with everything.

'I never thought that I would see this house again,' she remarked. 'I shall die happy.'

'Well, wait a while,' suggested her son. 'I'll be getting some more sheep, and you'll need to know how the lambing goes. Angus is coming back, remember him? He still has Shep, too. He can have the cottage at the end of the bottom drive. Donald wasn't interested in the fishing—I'm looking forward to that, there should be plenty of trout and salmon at the right time.'

They settled down to a pleasant discussion about the estate; it was small, but now that there was money to spend on it it should, in time, provide a livelihood. That was all her father and mother wanted, Rosie knew—their old home and enough to keep it viable. She left them talking and went upstairs to unpack her grandmother's luggage.

It rained the next day, which didn't matter much, for the old lady was content to inspect the house from attic to cellar, poking her long straight nose into every cupboard and drawer, and when she had examined everything she sat down and reminisced until a rather late lunch. In the afternoon she rested while Rosie read aloud to her from *Hamish Brown's Mountain Walk*, being corrected when she mispronounced the Gaelic names of the mountains. It was a relief when the old lady dropped off to sleep.

The sun shone the next day, and Rosie spent the morning trundling her grandparent around the gardens and a little way down the drive towards the back entrance leading to the Oban road. There were two cottages a few hundred yards from the house; Old Robert lived in one, alone now that his wife was dead, looked after by his daughter who lived next door with her husband Hugh, who had worked all his life for the Macdonalds, and their brood of children. Meg worked in the house once or twice a week, but that had been difficult, for Donald Macdonald hadn't cared for the small creatures running around the kitchen and poking their noses into the kitchen garden. But now Mrs Macdonald wanted her back—there were several empty rooms behind the kitchen where the children could play, and the two elder ones could pick the soft fruit and the beans and peas. They would be going to school in September, anyway; their father would drive them there in the farm truck and fetch them at tea-time, so there would only be the two little ones.

Old Mrs Macdonald had known Old Robert and his family, and went happily enough with Rosie to arrange things with Meg. They had a cup of tea in the cottage while the old lady reminisced at some length. It passed the morning very well, and she was in an amiable frame of mind when they went back to the house for lunch. It was halfway through that meal that the phone rang, and Rosie got up to answer it.

'That will be your aunt Carrie,' declared her grandmother, 'with some problem which needs my advice. She is incapable of running a house, I do not know what will happen when she marries. Tell her to telephone me later, Rosie.'

Rosie had the receiver to her ear, she was smiling, and had gone a little pink. 'It's for me,' she said over her shoulder.

Sir Fergus's voice, decisive and matter-of-fact, said in her ear, 'Shall we walk tomorrow? I have an urge to take a look at Rannoch Moor. Will you be ready by nine o'clock? We'll drive as far as Rannoch Station, and leave the car there. I'll bring you back in time for supper—it's light until nine o'clock. I might even take you out to supper provided we haven't fallen out by then.' And at her quick-drawn breath he added, 'No, no, don't get uppity, I shall strive to be the soul of good nature. What do you intend to do with Granny?'

Rosie gave a chortle of laughter and turned it into a cough. 'I'll think of something. Shall I bring some sandwiches?'

'No need, I'll bring food with me. Till tomorrow, and don't keep me waiting.'

He rang off, and she said, 'Well, really...!'

Her mother and father continued their mild conversation as she sat down again, but her grandmother saw no reason why she shouldn't poke her nose into her granddaughter's business.

'Well, who was that?' she wanted to know.

'Oh, just a friend, Granny. Shall I get coffee, Mother?'

'Please dear, and tell Mrs MacFee that she can clear the table in five minutes, will you?'

With old Mrs Macdonald staying with them, they had abandoned their cosy lunches in the kitchen, and they drank their coffee in the drawing-room; it made extra work, especially as they were still getting settled in, but, as her mother had pointed out to her husband, his mother expected it, and it was only for a week. He had given in, for he was a good son even if he and the old lady didn't see eye to eye on certain matters. He engaged her in conversation now, and presently Rosie helped her up the stairs to her room and settled her down for her post-prandial nap, which left her free to run downstairs again before the old lady could think of anything else she might need while taking a rest on her bed.

'That was Sir Fergus,' she told her mother.

Mrs Macdonald had picked up her knitting, and forced herself to finish the row before saying in a mildly questioning voice, 'Yes, dear?'

Rosie perched on the edge of the large and rather shabby sofa, and said, 'You're dying to know, aren't you? Only, I couldn't say anything with Granny there. Well, he's asked me to spend the day walking with him tomorrow, and I said I would. He's coming for me at nine o'clock—he wants to drive to Rannoch Station and leave the car there.'

'What shall we do with your grandmother?' asked her father from behind his newspaper.

'Oh, Father, dear——'

He interrupted her. 'I have to go to Oban in the morning; I'll take her in with me, and I'll give her lunch at the Caledonian Hotel and bring her back in time for her nap. Then it will be your mother's turn.'

Rosie skipped over to kiss the top of his head. 'You really are a splendid pair. I'll do anything you want after tomorrow.'

The sky was overcast when she got out of bed in the morning; the clouds hung low over the hills encircling the house—it would surely rain before the day was out.

Rosie got into a denim skirt and a short-sleeved cotton shirt, and went down to help her mother get the breakfast.

A pity it wasn't a fine day, but even a heavy downpour wasn't going to dim her good spirits. She fed Hob and Simpkins, fed the hens, made toast, and presently sat down to make a good breakfast. She had just taken up her grandmother's tray when Sir Fergus arrived. She saw him drive up from the landing window, and stopped to have a good look. He appeared different, but then she had never seen him dressed casually. Cavalry twill trousers, she guessed from her vantage-point, and a cotton sweater over an open-necked shirt. He looked younger. She went on down to the kitchen, regretting that her cotton shirt had no style to it at all.

He was in the kitchen, sitting on the table, drinking the coffee her mother had given him and eating the last of the breakfast toast, heavily buttered.

'Fergus left very early this morning; he didn't have a proper breakfast,' explained her mother as Rosie went in.

He got off the table and came to meet her. 'Hello. A good day for a tramp. I've brought Gyp with me; she likes a good walk.'

'Gyp?'

'My dog. You won't mind a few spots of rain?' He eyed her person in a leisurely manner. 'You're sensibly dressed, anyway. Better bring a jacket.'

'I have one ready,' said Rosie coldly. He sounded just as she imagined an elder brother would sound. It was obvious to her that the cotton shirt would be quite adequate; indeed, an old sack would have done just as well.

'Unless you would care for another slice of toast, I will get my jacket,' she told him.

He was standing by the car talking to her father when she got down. Gyp, a labrador with soulful eyes, was wandering around and came to meet her but, at a brief whistle from his master, got back into the car.

'Ready?' Sir Fergus bade her father goodbye, waved to her mother, who was standing at a window, and ushered her into the seat beside him.

'Enjoy your day,' said her father. She hoped that she would, but she wasn't sure.

Her doubts were quickly put at rest; her companion was at his most charming. 'A pity about this drizzle, but we may be lucky and get better weather later on.'

'I rather like sombre weather,' commented Rosie. 'Does Gyp like walking?'

'Loves it. Shall we have coffee at Rannoch? There's a picnic of sorts in the boot.'

'I should like that. Which way are we walking?'

'I thought the West Highland walkway for a start, but we can turn off on to the edge of the moor—it'll be pretty damp——' He glanced at her shoes. 'Sensible shoes, I see.'

To which she made no reply. Did he think that she was fool enough to wear something dainty with a high heel? And she born and brought up in the Highlands?

He went on smoothly, 'I have before now escorted ladies who had no idea how wild and remote the moor is. You know it well, I expect?'

'I've walked there several times with Father—the heather was out and the pools sparkled...'

'A bit early for the heather yet, but even under a grey sky the pools are a delight.'

'I'd love to skate across it . . .'

'We shall do it together next winter—much more fun than swimming across in the summer.'

'I've never met anyone who has done that.'

'Several of us did it—oh, years ago when we were medical students.'

'Was it very long ago?' she asked.

'I have been qualified for eleven years. I'm thirty-five, Rosie. Does that seem old to you?'

'Heavens, no! I'm twenty-five, you know.'

'Yes. I do know.' They were almost at Rannoch, and the Grampians loomed all around them.

'It's going to clear,' said Sir Fergus, and stopped outside the hotel.

They had their coffee, Gyp had a bowl of water, and they were on their way, sandwiches stashed away in pockets with a couple of bottles of spa water.

They took a track across the moor towards the twin peaks of Buachaille, and then doubled back to the road again. They were on the highest part of the moor now, and although the sky was cloud-filled the view was magnificent.

They found a fallen tree, and sat down on it and pointed out the various peaks to each other. 'I could sit here all day,' declared Rosie.

'Well, you're not going to. There's a stalker's path which will take up to Cashlie Station, and another one which will bring us out at Loch Tulla. We can pick up the road there.' He gave her a sidelong look. 'Not too far for you?'

'Certainly not, Sir Fergus.'

'Would it be possible for you to call me Fergus? We can find somewhere by Loch Tulla to eat our sandwiches.'

There was a strong, cool wind blowing, and Rosie, tramping along, her hair all over the place, her cheeks glowing, hadn't felt as happy for a long time; and she had never looked so pretty. The professor observed her discreetly, and decided that she was beautiful.

They walked on for some time until, at length, they saw the loch ahead of them.

'Good, I'm famished!' said the professor. 'There's a dead root over there; it will do nicely.'

So they sat eating their sandwiches—smoked salmon, cold beef, cheese and pickles, between thinly cut bread, lavishly buttered. 'Did you get these at the Hospital?' asked Rosie, her mouth full.

'No. My housekeeper rather fancies herself as a sandwich-maker.' He opened one of the bottles. 'You'll have to drink from it.'

Which she did with the unselfconsciousness of a child.

After a moment she asked, 'Are you married, Fergus?'

'You asked me that, or had you forgotten? Or perhaps I didn't give you a very satisfactory answer?'

'Well, you said that you hoped to be. I—I just wondered if you'd got married since then?'

He handed her a sandwich, the gleam in his eyes hidden. 'I'll let you know when I do marry, Rosie!'

CHAPTER SIX

THEY started walking again presently, and Fergus kept their talk impersonal, but after a while Rosie blurted out, 'I'm sorry, that was rude of me—asking you about being married, I mean. Of course, you couldn't possibly be, for if you were you wouldn't be here now, would you?'

He suppressed a smile, his voice matter-of-fact. 'Well, no. I rather think that when I marry I shall settle down and be an exemplary husband.'

She nodded. 'Well, yes, and anyway, I expect you have to be circumspect don't you—being well-known and respected?'

He threw back his head and let out a roar of laughter. 'Are you crediting me with leading a secretly amorous life behind the façade of my profession?'

She stopped, stamped her foot in temper, and got it wet. 'Now look what you've made me do—and what a silly thing to say! That wasn't what I meant at all—you know it wasn't.'

He said blandly, 'Well, of course I know; I cannot imagine why you should have any interest in me as a person. We scarcely know each other, do we?'

She looked up into his quiet face. 'No—no, we don't.'

'That can, of course, be remedied. Indeed, I thought that we were verging on a kind of cautious friendship.'

She smiled suddenly. 'Yes—well——' she put out a hand '—all right, Fergus.'

His hand was firm and very large, and for some reason she wanted to leave her own hand in its grasp. She withdrew it prudently, and he bent and kissed her gently.

'Sealed with a kiss,' he observed cheerfully. 'Let us walk on.'

Which they did.

Presently Rosie asked, 'It doesn't mean that we can't argue, does it?'

He smiled. 'My dear girl, if you should feel the urge to speak your mind, feel free to do so.'

'Oh, good. May I ask you about your work now without being nosy?'

'I'm an orthopaedic surgeon.'

'Yes, but everyone seems to know you—are you a consultant surgeon or something?'

'A consultant, yes. I have my base, so to speak, at the Royal Infirmary, but I visit other hospitals.'

'Hospitals in Scotland? They knew you at Oban.'

He said gravely, 'I go there from time to time. I go to England quite often. I went to Holland last week...'

'To a hospital? To operate?'

'Yes, and also to examine medical students.'

'Why were you knighted?'

'Oh, my name must have come first out of the hat.'

She, aware that he wasn't going to say more than that, asked, 'Am I asking too many questions?'

'No, no. They will clear the ground.'

It was on the tip of her tongue to ask what ground, but she suspected that if she did so he would only give her another puzzling reply.

They were back on the road again, skirting the moor, and after a time they reached the hotel once more. It was beginning to drizzle again, but the clouds were broken.

'It will be a fine day tomorrow,' Sir Fergus remarked. 'You'll be back in Edinburgh?'

'I'm driving down to Leeds and then on to London—I'll be away for quite a while.' He added idly, 'You are driving your granny back, I suppose?'

'Oh, yes, and I said I'd stay a couple of days so that my aunt Carrie can finish the plans for her wedding.'

He whistled to Gyp, and opened the hotel door. 'Tea, I think, don't you?'

'Yes, please.' She nodded briskly at him, and went off to look for the 'Ladies'; she must look pretty wind-swept and damp by now.

They ate a huge tea—buttered toast, sandwiches, scones and butter and almost all of a plate of cakes, sitting opposite each other at a small table in the hotel's cosy lounge with Gyp between them, enjoying her share.

'Have you been to Strontian? There's a good hotel there by the loch. Will you have dinner with me there?'

'Oh, yes, thank you.' And then, 'Will they let us in?' She looked down at her sensibly clad person. 'It's at the other end of Glen Tarbet, isn't it?'

'Yes—used a good deal by walkers and anglers. I don't think they'll object to us.' He glanced at his watch. 'They don't serve dinner after half-past seven, so perhaps we had better be going. We'll have to go up to Fort William and then down the other side of Loch Linnhe.'

'You've been there before?'

'Several times. On second thoughts we'll cross over at Ballachulish and get the ferry over to Corran, go down the 861 and turn off for Glen Tarbet. We may have to go back through Fort William, the ferry may not be running; it will have to be the long way round.'

'It's not all that far,' said Rosie instantly, so that he smiled to himself.

The road was a good one, running between the mountains, and the sky, washed clear of clouds once more, promised a magnificent sunset. They didn't talk much; Fergus, Rosie had discovered, wasn't a man who needed to be entertained with small talk. So beyond pointing out the occasional red deer or a particularly splendid waterfall or view she maintained the silence, and he made no attempt to break it.

The light was still good as he turned into Glen Tarbet; mountains towered to left and right of them, and then thick black forest which presently allowed them a glimpse of the loch ahead of them. The road narrowed as they entered the village and drove on for a short distance to the hotel. It was charming, standing in its own grounds bordering the loch, and any fears Rosie had about the wrong clothes were put at rest by their warm welcome. Sir Fergus, it seemed, was known there. She went away to make the best of her appearance, and joined him in the bar before they went in to dinner.

The hotel was quite full, and thankfully there were several parties dining who were wearing clothes as casual as her own. She settled down into her chair and cast an appreciative eye over the menu. She hadn't felt particularly hungry, but the menu was mouth-watering; she chose smoked salmon, roast beef and all the trimmings that went with it, and happily drank the claret Sir Fergus chose. She finished the meal with *millefeuille*, rejecting with regret his offer of a second helping, and then joining him for coffee.

They lingered over their meal, and the long evening was sliding into night when they left the hotel with Gyp walking sedately at her master's heels. Rosie perched on a nearby wall while Sir Fergus opened a box in the boot, arranged a bowl of food for Gyp and another bowl with water, and went to sit by her.

'Time for a stroll down to the Loch?' he enquired. 'It's half an hour to the ferry, and another forty minutes or so to Inverard.'

They sat for a while, and then walked slowly down to the water while Gyp wandered round, to come presently at his low whistle and get back into the car where she curled up and composed herself for a nap.

Sir Fergus glanced over his shoulder at the dog as he started up the engine. 'She's tired; what about you, Rosie?'

'Tired? Me? Not a bit—well, my feet are a bit, but I could go on all night like this . . .' She stopped abruptly, glad that he couldn't see her red face. 'What I mean . . .' she began, and wondered how to go on.

He helped her out with casual ease. 'I know exactly how you feel—there's a kind of magic about this part of the world, isn't there? I can understand why thousands come back year after year just to walk and climb. Do you climb, Rosie?'

They were driving back through Glen Tarbet, and the powerful car lights picked out the road ahead with rough grass slopes edging their way up to the mountains.

'No,' said Rosie, 'I'm frightened of heights. Silly, isn't it? Because I love the hills and mountains. I expect you climb, don't you?'

'Whenever I have the chance, which isn't very often.'

'Of course there isn't much chance if you live in Edinburgh!'

Fergus thought of his home, not so far away from where they were, surrounded by the highland hills and the loch close by. It wasn't the time to tell her about it; she must be given the chance to like him without any inducement to do so, not that he thought her likes and dislikes could be swayed by anyone once she had made up her mind. He smiled to himself in the dimness of the car, and said, 'Here we are at the ferry, and it's still running.'

He kept the conversation casual and undemanding for the rest of their journey, and it was Rosie who asked, as he turned the car through the open gates leading to her home,

'Do you have to leave in the morning? Won't you be tired? It's more than a hundred miles to Edinburgh...'

They could see the lights of her home twinkling at the bottom of the lane. 'You'll come in for coffee, won't you?'

'Is it not too late? It's kind of you to ask me, but I think I had better drive on.'

All the same, he got out of the car, and helped her out before doing the same for Gyp. The door opened at her touch, and she led the way into the drawing-room, to find her mother and father sitting there.

Her mother came to meet them. 'Have you had a lovely day? Fergus, you'll have coffee—it's all ready?'

He refused with charm and real regret. 'I have several matters to clear up before I leave in the morning. Perhaps you will invite me again?'

Mrs Macdonald said warmly, 'Of course—come whenever you like, don't wait to be asked. I think you work too hard.'

He shook hands and said goodbye, and Rosie went to the door with him.

'It was a lovely day; thank you very much, Fergus. I hope you have a successful trip.'

She didn't want him to go, and she very much wanted to know how long he had to be away for, but his brisk, 'A splendid day, Rosie, thank you for coming,' precluded any questions. She said goodbye, and he whistled to Gyp, got into the car, and drove away without a backward glance.

Somehow it wasn't quite how the day should have ended. Probably he had seen enough of her—it had been a mistake to have gone to Strontian for dinner.

'Over-exposure,' muttered Rosie. 'If he invites me out again—*if*—I must be doing something else.'

She went indoors and drank the coffee her mother had poured, described her day with a wealth of detail about the scenery, and presently she went to bed. Fergus would just about be in Edinburgh, she reflected as she curled up with Simpkins lolling over her feet. She wondered where he lived—Moray Place, perhaps, where the hierarchy of the medical profession lived? Or Belgrave Crescent? But that was further away from the Royal Infirmary... She went to sleep trying to decide.

He lived in Moray Place in a Georgian house facing the circular gardens at its centre. It had been his grandfather's house, and his mother had inherited it and handed it over to him, since she had no wish to leave her home by Loch Eilt. He had always enjoyed visiting his mother's parents when he was a small boy, and he had learned to love the house. He had changed very little since he had lived there, beyond turning powder closets into bathrooms and updating the kitchen and its adjacent rooms so that Mrs Meikle had all the modern equipment she could want. She had been with the family for as long as he could remember, and ran his household to perfection; and if she sometimes wished to return to her native Highlands she never said so. She had family living at Glenfinnan, and he often took her with him when he went to his home so that she might visit them.

He let himself into the silent house through its handsome painted front door, stopped in the long narrow hall to collect the letters waiting for him on a carved table, and went to his study. It was a large room, lined with books, and furnished comfortably with leather armchairs and a vast desk. He settled down in the big chair behind it, and poured himself coffee from the Thermos jug on a tray; there were sandwiches, too, and he picked one up, gave the crusts to Gyp, and munched the rest while he sorted his letters. There were telephone messages waiting for him. He rang the hospital and talked to the surgical officer on duty, and then to the night sister on the orthopaedic ward, and then went slowly through his letters, making notes for his secretary, and at the very end there was a note in Mrs Meikle's round hand, urging him to get a decent night's sleep, and telling him that she would see that he was called in good time in the morning.

He smiled at that, and an hour later did as she had bidden him.

* * *

Old Mrs Macdonald was cantankerous the next day. She had missed Rosie, she grumbled, and it was to be hoped that she wouldn't be left all alone all day again. Since she had spent a pleasant morning with her son, been given lunch by him, and spent the afternoon with her daughter-in-law, poking in cupboards and drawers and making arbitrary suggestions as to the rearrangement of the furniture throughout the entire house, her grumbles were unfounded. Rosie listened with a patient ear, trundled her grandparent around the garden, and allowed her thoughts to wander.

She had enjoyed her day with Fergus; they liked the same things and shared the same views. She had started off by not liking him, but now she had to admit that she liked him very much; it would be nice to know a great deal more about him—his work and his home and friends. It wasn't very likely that she would, though. He had volunteered very little about himself—only that one casual remark that he hoped to marry soon... The very idea saddened her so that her grandmother, pausing in her diatribe concerning modern youth, wanted to know what was the matter.

'You look as though you had lost your last sixpence,' she remarked acidly. 'You young people are never content—always wanting something you can't have.'

'Don't worry, Granny. I've all I want and I'm quite content.'

Which remark she had to admit to herself wasn't quite true.

The remaining days of her grandmother's visit passed pleasantly enough; it was almost as if Uncle Donald had never lived at Inverard. The old lady refused to talk about it or him; instead she discussed the running of the place

with her son, reminisced about her own life when she
had lived there, and wasted a good deal of her daughter-
in-law's time giving unwanted advice. Rosie came in for
her share too. Why had she not married? Where were
all the young men who should be courting her? And
what did she intend to do? Stay for the rest of her life
dwindling into an old maid?

To all of which Rosie replied suitably and with great
patience. She was fond of the old lady, but a little of
her went a long way; it was with well-concealed relief
that she settled her grandmother in the back of the car
and prepared to drive her back to Edinburgh.

Rosie was wearing one of her new dresses and elegant
high-heeled sandals. It would probably rain later in the
day, and she had prudently stowed a mac in the boot
with her overnight bag, but since she would be in
Edinburgh for two days it was a splendid chance to air
at least some of her new wardrobe. Not that there was
anybody to notice it. By anybody she meant Sir Fergus,
of course, although she didn't admit that even to herself.

Edinburgh was crowded with tourists, but the street
where her grandmother lived was quiet enough. She
parked the car in front of the door, helped the old lady
out, and handed her over to the waiting Elspeth, and
went to unload the boot. Before she went indoors she
couldn't resist looking up and down the street. Sir Fergus
had driven down it once; he might do so again. There
was, however, no sign of the Rolls-Royce, and she went
into the house feeling quite unreasonably disappointed.

Her grandmother declared that she was exhausted; she
had to be revived with tea, then helped to her bed, and
given time to have a nap before dinner. Rosie unpacked
her few odds and ends, and went downstairs to help

Elspeth lay the table. It had begun to rain, but rain or
no rain she would have liked a walk. She stared out of
the window at the wet pavements, and thought longingly
of Rannoch Moor and its pools and marshes and lonely
splendour. She wouldn't want to live in Edinburgh—at
least, it might be all right if one were married with a
husband and children and a house to run, and perhaps
a weekend cottage in the Highlands, which naturally
enough led her thoughts to the whereabouts of Sir Fergus
and where he lived.

It was raining quite hard now, and the traffic was
sparse and slow so that she had ample time to see the
Rolls-Royce sliding past with Sir Fergus at the wheel and
a remarkably handsome woman sitting beside him. If
he saw her car parked—and he must have done for he
had to drive round it—he gave no sign. He gave no sign
of having seen her standing so plainly at the window
either, but then he was a man adept at concealing his
thoughts and feelings under a bland expression.

Rosie flounced away from the window, and Elspeth,
coming into the room, said, 'Och, and what's upset ye,
lassie?'

'Nothing—nothing at all, Elspeth. I was just thinking
that I would very much dislike living in Edinburgh.' She
rearranged a fork or two. 'I'll get Granny up, shall I?
She'll have an appetite for the dinner you've cooked.'

Her grandmother was in a mellow mood; the food
was good, and Elspeth had taken care to set her favourite
dishes on the table. They had their coffee at the table,
and then went into the drawing-room to play cards until
the old lady declared that she was ready for bed.

As Rosie bade her goodnight, having seen her into
bed, and fetched the hand-bell in case of need in the

night, fetched some fresh water and the book she wished to read should she not sleep, and then got the smelling-salts in case she felt faint, her grandmother observed, 'I shall have my breakfast in bed in the morning, and have a good rest. You may go shopping for Elspeth, Rosie; it will give her more time to look after me. She can make out a list for you—your aunt Carrie is a fool in a super-market, and it is a good opportunity to stock up while she is away from home.'

Rosie, her thoughts still chasing each other around her head, said, 'Yes, Granny,' with unwonted meekness, and went to her own bed. She might just as well spend the day in some supermarket, for there was no prospect of anything more exciting. She pummelled her pillows and curled up in the high old-fashioned bed.

'I hope I never see him again,' she muttered and, just before she slept, 'I shall go to Oban and let Dr Douglas know that we are at Inverard.'

She ate her breakfast with Elspeth in the kitchen, helped her wash the dishes, and studied the list of groceries she was to buy. It appeared to be a long list—she would never be able to carry all the things on it—and there was nowhere to park the car near the shopping centre.

'I shall take a taxi back,' she told Elspeth. 'How on earth does aunt Carrie manage?'

She didn't wait for an answer, but went to get her handbag and a couple of shopping baskets. It was a fine morning and still early; at least the walk would be pleasant enough.

She was crossing a street, intent on getting to the supermarket, when Sir Fergus saw her while he waited for the lights to change. He parked the car and headed for the nearest supermarket; Rosie had been burdened with two baskets, and it seemed the most likely place to look.

Rosie, pushing a trolley and eyeing her list with an impatient eye, was loading flour and sugar when she was halted by a large hand on hers. She knew whose hand it was because she was experiencing a very pleasant sensation at its touch.

She was unable to stop going pink, but she said with commendable coolness, 'Good morning, Sir Fergus—one would hardly expect to find you in a supermarket.'

He ignored that. 'I'll push this thing, you throw in whatever is on that list; we can be out of here in ten minutes...'

She stood facing him, still holding on to the trolley. 'I have to take it back to Granny's house.'

'Of course you do. We'll put it all in the boot and have coffee somewhere first, shall we?'

'Aren't you working today?'

'Not until this afternoon.'

'Well, don't you want to be with—with someone else?' Her voice was tart, and he glanced at her, smiling a little.

'No. Give me that list—I'll read it out, and you fling the stuff in.'

He took the trolley from her. 'Baking powder, white pepper, cooking salt...'

There was no use in arguing with him; they went up and down the aisles loading the trolley.

'Fairy... What in...?'

'Washing powder.'

'Domestos, Flash, scouring powder...'

Fergus handed back the list. 'Do you like shopping in these places?'

She shook her head. 'No, of course I don't; I like village shops where one can have a good gossip and watch the bacon being sliced...'

They joined a queue, and he began to unload the shopping, and that done took her baskets from her and went to the end of the counter to load them up. When she had paid and joined him he asked, 'And who does this when you're not here?'

'Aunt Carrie or Elspeth.'

'Tradespeople call, surely?'

They most certainly would for him, she reflected. 'Oh, yes, some of the grocers still deliver, but Granny says this is cheaper.'

He led her outside. 'Where are we going?'

'To the car.'

He loaded the baskets into the boot, and opened the door for her to get in. Rosie said, 'I'm sure Granny will be glad to give you coffee.'

'I thought we might drive out to Aberdour, the coffee at the Woodside Hotel is excellent.'

'But that's about twenty miles...'

For answer he picked up the car phone. 'What is your grandmother's number?' When she told him he dialled it.

'I spoke to Elspeth, and she will tell Mrs Macdonald that you will be back in time for lunch.'

Rosie had listened to his brief conversation with her pretty mouth ajar. 'Whatever will Granny say? She expects me back.'

'For lunch, Rosie; it's a pity I have a list at one o'clock otherwise we could have had lunch too.'

He was driving through the city, avoiding the main roads and coming finally to the Forth Bridge, not talking at all, which she found unnerving, so that halfway over the bridge she blurted out, 'I saw you in your car yesterday. Was that your fiancée with you?'

'Grizel? A handsome woman, is she not?' He spoke carelessly, and it was obvious to her that that was the only answer he was going to give her. Which served her right for being a Nosy Parker. She looked out of the window.

'The country is very pretty along this coast, isn't it?'

He didn't bother to answer that. 'When do you go back to Inverard?'

'When Aunt Carrie comes back—tomorrow or the next day. Did you have a successful trip to Leeds and London?'

'Yes. Rosie, will you spend the day with me when I come up to the Highlands next week?'

Her heart gave a thump of delight, but she ignored that.

'That would have been nice, but I don't think so, thank you.'

'Spending your spare time with young Douglas?' he wanted to know casually.

'Yes, yes, I am. He's very nice.' She fibbed too quickly.

She peeped at Sir Fergus's profile; it looked as calm as it always did.

'It is kind of you to ask me.' Strong feelings got the better of good sense. 'You shouldn't; if I were going to marry you I would be extremely annoyed with you——' she gulped '—asking another girl out.'

'Ah, but you're very likely to marry young Douglas, aren't you?' He turned to smile at her. 'Which makes it all very correct and proper.'

This was uttered in a tone of calm logic which had the effect of allaying any qualms she might have had.

'Well, if you're sure it's all right, I—I would enjoy it.'

'Good. I'll give you a ring when you get home,' He added blandly, 'I don't imagine young Douglas would object?'

'No, no I'm sure he wouldn't.'

It was a pity, she thought worriedly, that she had saddled herself with Dr Douglas, who, for all she knew, might be on the point of marrying someone else. Not that Sir Fergus was ever likely to know that...

They had their coffee at the hotel and Rosie, lulled by her companion's cordial manner, forgot her faint doubts and enjoyed herself. It was a pity that they were not able to stay longer but, as Sir Fergus pointed out, her grandmother would be needing the groceries and his theatre sister would subject him to a tart telling-off if he were to be too late in Theatre.

Rosie took that with a pinch of salt; she couldn't imagine anyone daring to tell Sir Fergus off.

'What is she like, your theatre sister?' she wanted to know.

'Short and round with grey hair, black eyes and a tongue like a razor. I'm terrified of her!'

There was plenty to talk about on the way back, and the journey seemed far too short to Rosie. Sir Fergus stopped outside her grandmother's house, carried her shopping to the door for her, and then drove away as Elspeth opened it.

'Yer grandmother's in a fine tantrum,' said Elspeth. 'Ye'd best spend a wee while with her.'

Old Mrs Macdonald was in a peevish mood, and Rosie was hauled over the coals. She was an ungrateful girl, heartless and uncaring; moreover, she had very likely spent too much money on the groceries.

'The young woman of today...' began the old lady, and entered into a diatribe concerning the deplorable ways of the rising generation.

Rosie listened meekly while she thought about Sir Fergus.

Aunt Carrie came back the next day, but too late for Rosie to drive herself back to Inverard, so that she had to listen to a similar lecture directed at her aunt. Both of them listened with apparent attentiveness while Aunt Carrie pondered bedroom curtains and Rosie pondered Sir Fergus.

She left for home the next morning. It was raining again, but since it rained a great deal in that part of Scotland she hardly noticed it. She didn't hurry; even in the rain the scenery was magnificent, and she had a lot to think about—pleasant thoughts mainly concerned with what she would wear if and when Sir Fergus asked her out. Her choice would be limited if they were to go walking, although she had some new T-shirts. On the other hand, if her entertainment was to be rather more sophisticated, there were the summer dresses with their matching cardigans—not run-of-the-mill garments, but stylish jackets with embroidery which matched the dresses.

She had her clothes nicely sorted out by the time she reached home.

At the end of three days she wondered why she had bothered; Sir Fergus hadn't telephoned, and it was already 'next week'. On the fourth day she invented an excuse to go to Oban, and took herself off to Dr Douglas's surgery—ostensibly to let him know that her parents were now living at Inverard. That he already knew this was incidental to her visit, and gave him the opportunity to ask her out to lunch.

Over that meal she listened with flattering attention to his aims and ambitions, and agreed that Oban, while a good enough place, held very little challenge for a young man with ambition.

'I would prefer to go to London or Birmingham,' said Dr Douglas, 'and perhaps return to Edinburgh or Glasgow. There is always room for a good man.'

He was a nice young man, but Rosie was appalled to discover that she found him rather boring. How on earth had she allowed Sir Fergus to think that she was contemplating marriage with him? Not that it mattered, since Sir Fergus was contemplating marriage himself.

Sir Fergus telephoned that evening as she was laying the table for dinner. He sounded cheerful and far too casual, so that she found herself telling him that she had had a delightful time lunching with Dr Douglas.

She wished she hadn't mentioned it when he said cheerfully, 'Oh, good—the more you see of each other the better. Can he spare you tomorrow? I'll call for you about nine o'clock.'

'I'm not sure,' began Rosie with a touch of peevishness at being taken for granted, and then, anxious that he might accept this as a formal refusal, quickly agreed. 'Well, yes. Thank you. Are we going to walk?'

'Wait and see. Please don't keep me waiting.'

Upon which arbitrary note he rang off, leaving her put out. However, not so put out that she couldn't bend her mind to the important task of thinking of what to wear. A problem—if they weren't going for a tramp away from the roads she couldn't possibly wear a sensible skirt and shirt and stout shoes. Something that would pass muster whatever they did... She decided upon another new dress—a cotton jersey in a vague pink, very plain with a round neck and short sleeves and a swinging skirt; she could wear one of the new cardigans with it—a slightly darker pink, and plain. Tan sandals, flat-heeled and not too flimsy would be ideal.

'And it will be just too bad if he's planned some hike to some rugged mountain with the idea of making me climb it!' she observed to Simpkins, who was watching her from the comfort of her bed.

She went to tell her mother presently, and that lady said mildly, 'How nice, dear—such an opportunity to get out and about while we still have summer. Where are you going?'

'I don't know—he wouldn't say—I don't know what to wear.'

'Well, he seems a considerate man, love; if he planned a walk he would have told you.'

'I asked him if we were going to walk and he said "wait and see",' said Rosie with asperity.

'If he said that, then he has something planned; he wouldn't want you mincing along in flimsy shoes if he had a good hike in mind.'

Mrs Macdonald spoke placidly, and glanced at her beautiful daughter with a hopeful eye. Rosie seldom spoke of the professor, and her mother took that as a good sign—Fergus would be a delightful son-in-law, she reflected wistfully. It was a pity about this vague girl in the background, although she was shrewd enough to consider that probably Rosie had misunderstood him when he had mentioned getting married. She picked up her knitting, the picture of maternal calm.

'That's a pretty pink dress you brought back from Edinburgh—you could wear it anywhere,' she observed. 'But you'd better take a mac.'

Sir Fergus wasn't mentioned again. Rosie saw to the hens, collected the eggs, and went into the garden to get on with the weeding which Old Robert never had the time to do. It tired her out nicely so that by the time she went to bed any doubts she had about the next day were smothered in yawns and, presently, sound sleep.

It was a lovely morning; Rosie got up early, saw to the hens, and studied the sky. At the moment it looked as though it would be a fine day, and her spirits lifted. She enjoyed Fergus's company—she made no bones about admitting that now—but perhaps it would be as well if she didn't see any more of him after today. She went back indoors to get into the pink dress, and decided that she would concentrate on Dr Douglas.

Half an hour later, watching Fergus getting out of his car, she discovered that concentrating on Dr Douglas wasn't going to be the answer.

CHAPTER SEVEN

SIR FERGUS had Gyp with him; he crossed to the front door unhurriedly, wearing, Rosie was glad to note, clothes not suited to a day's hard walking. She was peeping from her bedroom window, and had plenty of time to appreciate the casual elegance of his clothes—he never seemed to wear anything new, she thought confusedly, but it always looked right . . .

He looked up suddenly and saw her, and stopped in his stride to look at her. It was a long, grave look, and it shook her to her bones so that she was incapable of moving away from his gaze. She wasn't sure how long they stood there, but it was her mother's voice that broke the spell.

Rosie retreated from the window, and took a look at herself in the looking-glass. She had the feeling that she was under a spell, but her face appeared to be the same as usual.

'If this is falling in love,' she observed to the faithful Simpkins, 'it is the most wonderful feeling; only, however am I going to go downstairs and talk to him as though nothing has happened?'

The longer she thought about it the worse it was going to be. She picked up her shoulder-bag, and went down to meet him.

His 'good morning, Rosie', was uttered with casual friendliness, so that for a moment she wondered if she had imagined his look and her sudden rush of feeling.

However, the feeling was still there; she would have liked to have run to him and flung herself into his arms and stayed there forever; she hadn't known that being in love could cause such chaos in an ordinary well-brought-up girl's head and heart. She bade him good morning in a carefully expressionless voice, not quite looking at him so that she didn't see the smile tugging at the corner of his mouth.

He said, 'You look nice—are you ready to go?'

'Yes. I'll just tell Mother.'

Mrs Macdonald came through the door like a stage character on cue.

'Fergus—how nice—I was in the kitchen—have you been here long?' She gave him a guileless smile and offered a hand, and he smiled gently down at her.

'A few minutes only.'

'You won't have coffee before you go?'

'It's such a lovely morning I feel we should take advantage of it.'

Mr Macdonald, coming in through the kitchen on his way to the study, came to join them in the hall. 'Fergus, good morning. You've chosen a splendid day, though it'll rain before night.'

The professor held out a hand. 'Good morning, sir. I'm afraid you may be right—as long as it holds off until evening.' He glanced at Rosie, standing very quietly. 'I hope Rosie will have dinner with me, so please don't worry if I bring her back rather late.'

'I have my key,' said Rosie, her voice faintly acid; just for the moment annoyance that he had taken it for granted that she would accept his invitation without, as it were, being asked, took over from her wish to spend every day with him forever and ever.

They were all looking at her.

The professor said in a voice to charm the birds off a tree, 'It would be a delightful end to the day if you would dine with me, Rosie?'

The smile with which he accompanied this invitation would have melted a stone.

'That would be nice,' replied Rosie, quite unable to resist the charm. 'I don't know where we're going—I'm not sure if I'm wearing...'

'Quite delightful,' interrupted Sir Fergus. 'Shall we get on?'

They said their goodbyes, Gyp clambered into the back of the car, and Rosie was ushered into the front seat. Then Sir Fergus turned the car and drove away up the long drive to the road.

'Where are we going?' asked Rosie.

'You know Loch Eilt?'

'I've seen it—I've never actually stopped by it. It looked lovely—all those little islands with those silvery trees... Is that where we're going?'

'Yes. Why did you look like that, Rosie?'

She knew quite well what he meant, but she asked, 'Like what?'

'As though you hadn't seen me before. We are moderately well acquainted, are we not?' When she stayed silent he observed, 'You don't wish to tell me, do you?'

'No, It wasn't because I wasn't glad to see you, though.'

'I'm glad to hear that.' He sent the car spinning along the road to Fort William. 'How is your friendship progressing with young Douglas?'

'Douglas? Oh, Dr Douglas. Oh, well...very nicely.'

If he considered her reply was less enthusiastic than was to be expected from a young woman cherishing thoughts of marriage he said nothing, but presently began a casual conversation about nothing much which lasted until they had left Fort William behind them and turned off on the road to Mallaig.

'Are we going to Skye?'

'No. Would you like to go there one day? Do you know it at all?'

'I've been several times, but I don't know the north of the island at all, though I've been to Kyle of Lochalsh—one could spend a lifetime here and never see it all.'

Rosie was making conversation, anxious to achieve a casual friendliness, and she was finding it difficult; besides, she was puzzled as to where he was taking her. They crossed the head of Loch Shiel and drove though Glenfinnan, and glimpsed Loch Eilt ahead of them. This was where he had said they would be going; she had her mouth open to ask him if this was where they would stop—for a picnic perhaps?—when he turned the car through the open gates and she saw the sign behind them.

'This is private,' she pointed out, turned to look at his placid profile; and at his laconic 'yes' she knew at last.

'You live here!' she said accusingly. 'You might have said so.'

He didn't answer, which annoyed her, and she stared out of the window with her beautiful nose in the air. When the house came in sight she forgot about being haughty.

'Oh, it's magnificent!' In her surprise and pleasure she put out a hand and clutched his sleeve, and then snatched it back as though she had touched a hot coal...

'Sorry,' she mumbled, and knew that she must seem an idiot to him, behaving like a silly schoolgirl.

Sir Fergus didn't look at her, nor did he speak for the moment, but drew up at the door before he turned to her. He said gently, 'I wanted to surprise you, Rosie.'

'You have. Oh, it's lovely; don't you want to live here all the time?'

He got out, opened her door and helped her out, and did the same for Gyp.

'Yes—it's my home, but if I lived here all the time I'd have to give up my work, and I couldn't do that.'

They were standing looking at the house, and Rosie said slowly, 'But when you marry will your wife live here? Isn't it too far for you to commute? Or perhaps she likes Edinburgh?'

He looked away from her. 'I hope that she will like to be with me wherever I am.' He added, 'Shall we go inside?'

Hamish had opened the door when they had arrived, and had stood well back watching them, nodding his old head in a satisfied way. Now he edged forward to bid them a good morning.

He took the hand Rosie offered, and his 'Guid day, Miss Macdonald' was uttered in a contented voice which made Sir Fergus grin.

'Is my mother in the drawing-room, Hamish?'

'The wee morning-room, ye ken fine she loves the roses.'

Sir Fergus led Rosie to the back of the hall, and opened a door opposite the sitting-room. It was a small room

with deep windows and doors opening on to the lawn
beyond, and Rosie could see why Hamish had mentioned roses—the velvety grass was surrounded by rose
beds filled to overflowing with every shade of pink, red
and yellow. Mrs Cameron was sitting in the doorway
with a book on her lap, but she got up as they went in.

'Fergus—and you have brought Rosie to meet me.'
She lifted a cheek for his kiss, and offered a hand to
Rosie, her smile very sweet. 'I am so delighted to meet
you; Fergus tells me that you are living at Inverard again.
You are glad to be back there?'

She patted the chair near hers. 'Come and sit down
and tell me about it—we'll have coffee before Fergus
carries you off.'

Gyp, with Bobby at his heels, came in from the garden,
and Mrs Cameron asked, 'You like dogs?'

She began to talk comfortably about the animals, the
garden and the delights of living almost on the shores
of the loch, with Sir Fergus putting in an easy word or
two, so that presently Rosie had the pleasant feeling that
she had known Mrs Cameron for quite some time, and
that sitting there with her and Fergus stretched out in
his big chair was something she had done for years instead of the few minutes she had been there.

Hamish brought in the coffee-tray, and presently
Fergus asked, 'Would you like to walk down to the loch?
We can go across the gardens, and come back through
the woods.'

The gardens were beautiful; beyond the roses was a
small walled garden with an herbaceous border in full
flower and then a little herb garden before they crossed
rough ground beneath the trees and came out by the loch.
Half a dozen miles away, on the further side of the loch,

the mountains towered, their lower slopes covered with fir trees, and merging into moorland already tinged with purple heather.

Sir Fergus flung an arm round Rosie's shoulders. 'Splendid, isn't it? I think of this when I'm in Edinburgh.'

She was very conscious of his arm. 'Do you come here each weekend?'

'Whenever I can—it isn't always possible; I have friends in Edinburgh—one doesn't like to lose touch.'

He glanced down at her. 'And you, Rosie? There must be old friendships for you now that you are back at Inverard—new ones, too?'

'Well, yes. It's as though we've never been away...'

'So you are content to stay at Inverard?'

If she said no he would want to know why, and how could she tell him that she would only be content to stay there if he were there too? She had never been a jealous girl, but now she experienced the first pangs at the thought of him far away in Edinburgh, surrounded by the flower of eligible womanhood ready to pounce if his matrimonial plans should come to grief.

'I'm not there all the time,' she pointed out in what she hoped was an uninterested manner. 'I go down to see Granny and Aunt Carrie, and I go shopping. Aunt Carrie is getting married in two weeks' time. She wants me to be her bridesmaid...'

'So it is to be a big wedding?' he asked idly.

'Oh, no! They're being married in Tron church. I'm not quite sure why; I believe they first met there, or something like that. It's to be very quiet.'

'Your aunt deserves to be happy; I should imagine that your grandmother isn't the easiest of women to live with.'

'She's not.' Rosie gave a little chortle of laughter. 'Aunt Carrie is a saint, and so kind; but we all take it in turns to be out of favour with Granny; she forgives us sooner or later—all except Uncle Donald.'

'Does she approve of your marrying young Douglas?'

She did a quick think—it was important to give the right answer. 'Well, I don't think she knows yet.'

'Ah, a secret romance...' There was mockery in his voice so that she answered before she had time to think.

'Good heavens, no—he hasn't a spark of romance in him!'

She could have bitten out her tongue. She went red, and added hastily, 'Well, you know what men are...'

He quelled silent laughter. 'Er—yes, but only from a man's point of view, of course.'

He slid an arm under hers, and began to walk in the direction of the lochside.

'Just because young Douglas doesn't quote Robbie Burns to you doesn't mean to say that he doesn't think it. "To see her is to to love her and love but her and her for ever, for Nature made her what she is and never made anither".'

He said the words in broad Scots, and Rosie longed with all her heart that he had quoted the poem just for her. He hadn't, of course; he would have been thinking of his future wife. The thought made her uneasy; here they were, walking along arm-in-arm, very much at ease with each other indeed—even when he annoyed her the annoyance didn't touch her deep love for him, and that wouldn't do at all...

She apologised silently to the unknown girl who had his heart, and said briskly, 'Ian would like to get a partnership in Edinburgh.'

He had mentioned it casually to her when she had gone to see him; what he hadn't mentioned was that he wanted her to go with him. But there was no need to tell Fergus that. Ian Douglas was a nice young man, but he wasn't serious about her; he was prudent enough to marry a girl with money and good connections. True, she had the connections, but there was no money to spare; her father intended to spend every penny on getting Inverard back on to its feet again. Fergus wasn't to know that, and she would take care to see that he never did.

'That shouldn't be too difficult. Shall I keep an eye open for him? I have contacts with most of the medical men there?'

'I'll ask him. Do you have a practice, or do you just work at the hospital?'

He was still holding her arm. 'Oh, I have a practice, quite a busy one. Of course I work at the hospital too—two lists each week and outpatients and an after-care clinic. I have a registrar and several housemen, and I take a teaching round...'

'You can't have a minute to yourself...'

He laughed. 'My registrar is my right arm; he takes over and two of the housemen at least are more than competent. They need to be, for I am away from time to time.'

'You went to Holland?'

'Yes—I go quite frequently. I go to London, Birmingham, Leeds and Bristol, too.'

She spoke without remembering to curb her tongue. 'You'll never have any time to be at home. Won't your wife mind?' She added, 'When you're married.'

'I shall take her with me. If we walk a little further there is an old stone hut—I considered it mine when I was a boy. It is overgrown with trees and shrubs, and it is a splendid hideaway.'

'How interesting,' commented Rosie, feeling snubbed. He considers that we are friends, she thought crossly, but if I ask questions about his life and what he does he slams the door in my face.

She added defiantly, 'Ian is most interested in old buildings.'

Which was a fib thought up on the spur of the moment.

All in a good cause, she reflected, crossing her fingers behind her back.

The hut, when they reached it, *was* interesting—a kind of look-out post on the curve of the loch. It was roofless, and over the years trees had grown in and around it, almost screening the small openings which took the place of windows.

'I used to shoot with my bow and arrow through them,' observed Sir Fergus. He put a remembering hand on the rough stonework. 'And later on my father gave me an air-gun—I taught myself to shoot here.'

Rosie didn't speak; she was afraid that if she did he might stop talking—such a small scrap of information, but she treasured it. However, it was all she was going to get.

He gazed at his watch, and said, 'We had better stroll back, lunch is at one o'clock.'

They ate it in a large square room overlooking the grounds and, beyond, the loch. The room was panelled with light oak, and the ceiling was of elaborate plaster-work. The dining table was rectangular, ringed by leather-seated chairs of the Regency period. There was a vast sideboard and a splendid marble fireplace with a mirror above. The table had a white damask cloth, and the porcelain plates and dishes were blue and white, the remnants of a vast service sent over from China some hundred and fifty years previously, each bearing the family coat-of-arms.

Lunch did justice to its elegant surroundings—smoked salmon, trout, a salad, and strawberry tartlets with lashings of cream. Rosie, who had a healthy appreciation of good food, enjoyed every mouthful. She enjoyed the conversation, too, although never once did Sir Fergus allow her an insight into his life.

Why should he? she reflected, drinking coffee in the drawing-room, its grandeur softened by chintz-covered armchairs and sofas, and the vast dim pink carpet on its floor. There were vitrines on either side of the enormous window, filled with miniature silver and porcelain, and two small tables—Dutch marquetry on rosewood. There were elaborate gilt sconces on either side of the fireplace, and an ornate crystal chandelier hung from the ceiling. The room's grandeur was further domesticated by Bobby and Gyp, who had flung themselves down on the carpet, a pile of magazines and books on one of the tables, and a half-knitted garment cast down on one of the chairs. It was a lovely room, and lived in; Rosie would have liked to have seen the rest of the house, but Sir Fergus put down his cup and said,

'I have to go to Arisaig—just to cast an eye on a patient of mine. Come with me, Rosie?'

It was a beautiful drive—alongside the loch for a good deal of the way until they glimpsed the sea and the islands beyond on their right, and presently reached the village. Arisaig House stood in the grounds which swept down to the loch, and stood surrounded by mountains.

'It's an hotel,' observed Rosie unnecessarily.

'Yes—and a very nice one, too. One of the boys broke a leg a couple of months ago—I took the plaster off last week, and I want to make sure that he's not running races on it.'

He swept the car up to the door, and several people came out to meet them—a large and cheerful family, all talking at once. Rosie, introduced simply as Rosie Macdonald, found herself surrounded by a group of children, one of them with a crutch. They all went back indoors, through the hotel foyer to the private wing, where she was invited to sit down, and submitted to a friendly cross-examination while the boy with the crutch was led away by Sir Fergus and his mother.

There were five children, their father and an aunt left to entertain her. The talk was generally impersonal for a start, but the children were full of questions. Where did she live? Had she a horse of her own? Did she like dogs? Was she going to marry Fergus?'

It was unfortunate that this last question was fired at her just as Sir Fergus returned, and while she might have been able to ignore it and hope that no one had heard it the aunt spoilt it all by saying in a clear voice,

'That is rude, Robert—you mustn't ask Rosie if she is going to marry Sir Fergus.'

There was a lull in the conversation so that everyone in the room heard her. Rosie went delightfully pink and looked at her feet; she would have to say something...

Sir Fergus spoke instead. A perfectly natural question,' he observed blandly, 'but I wouldn't ask if I were you, Robert; you would be jumping the gun.'

'What's jumping the gun?' asked Robert, instantly diverted.

'Oh, lord, what have I started?' The professor went on to explain patiently with great good humour, and by the time he had finished Rosie's colour was normal again and she was being borne off to the enormous kitchen to have tea.

They all sat round the big table while a stout elderly woman they addressed as Nanny poured tea, admonished the children from time to time, and handed scones and cake, jam and honey. Rosie, with the lady of the house beside her and one of the smaller daughters on the other side, began to enjoy herself. They were such a happy family, and she had been absorbed into it with instant ease. As for Sir Fergus, he was sitting opposite her, eating any number of scones and illustrating something with teaspoons and the bread-and-butter plate on the scrubbed table. He will make a marvellous father, thought Rosie, suddenly sad at the thought.

They left presently, and she was sorry to go, but the hotel had to be run, and there were certain duties waiting.

'Do come again,' they begged her. 'It's such an easy run for Fergus—he can bring you for a meal...'

Rosie thanked her hostess, and murmured vaguely. Of course he could bring her for a meal, but would he want to? He would more likely wish to bring the girl he was going to marry. She wondered if he had done so already, and on their way back she asked, 'Do you often go there? They're awfully nice...'

'I've known them for years, and since there are six children I've had arms and legs to deal with from time to time. I'm glad you liked them.'

'Do you—that is, have you...?'

He turned to grin at her. 'Oh, yes, once—we had a delightful time. Presently he asked, 'Should I feel flattered at your interest in my private life, Rosie?'

'I am not in the least interested!'

He said coolly, 'Well, you have no reason to be, have you? And when you are married to your Ian you will forget me until such time as you should break a leg or invite me to set a child's arm or collar-bone.'

She looked away so that he shouldn't see the sudden threat of tears.

Presently she said, rather too brightly, 'They are charming children—it must be delightful to be one of a large family.'

After that they fell into a silence broken only by a desultory remark from Sir Fergus from time to time, and when they got back to the house his mother was there waiting for them in the sitting-room and the talk became general until they were summoned to dinner.

Before that Rosie had had her chance to see something of the house, for her hostess had led her upstairs to tidy herself, and shown her into a charmingly furnished room with a rose-patterned wallpaper and little canopied bed. She had sat herself down before the old-fashioned looking-glass and studied her face as she powdered it. It surprised her that her sadness didn't show.

They dined in a leisurely fashion; cock a leekie soup, shoulder of lamb carved by the masterly hand of Sir

Fergus, a variety of vegetables grown, Mrs Cameron observed, in their own kitchen gardens, and a dream of a trifle. They talked about a great many things, but never anything remotely connected with Sir Fergus.

They sat over their coffee, and a pleasant hour had slipped by before Rosie saw the time.

'Heavens, it's late—I'm so sorry, I should have noticed.' She added ingenuously, 'I have enjoyed myself.'

'So have I, Rosie; you must come again.' Mrs Cameron smiled warmly as she spoke.

Sir Fergus said nothing at all, only got up as Rosie got to her feet.

'You're going back to Edinburgh?' she asked as she got into the car.

'Tomorrow.'

'But if you drive me home you won't be back here for hours!'

'A little more than an hour to Inverard, and a little more than an hour back here. I like driving at night.'

They turned to wave to Mrs Cameron standing at the open door, and the car shot away smoothly along the drive and on to the empty road.

Sir Fergus drove fast, but never recklessly. What traffic there was had died down; he slowed from time to time for sheep, and once to direct a tourist driving to Mallaig, and he talked about this and that in an easy manner, friendly and impersonal. She could have been an aunt he was being polite to for his mother's sake, Rosie thought with something like despair.

She sat there beside him making suitable replies to his remarks and pondered the fact that convention prevented her from uttering what her heart wished to say.

Although that, she reminded herself sensibly, would have embarrassed him and put an end to their friendship.

There was only a dim light in the hall when they arrived at Inverard. So Fergus got out of the car and opened her door, and she stood beside him for a moment, looking up at the sleeping house.

'Would you like to come in for coffee? Mother will have left something...'

He shook his head. 'It is late, and I have to be up early in the morning. Is the door locked?'

'No. Thank you for a lovely day; I have enjoyed it.'

He walked with her to the door and opened it for her. 'Lock it after you.'

'Yes, although there is no need here, you know.' She put out a hand. 'Goodnight, Fergus.'

He took her hand and held it, and bent and kissed her with a swift gentleness. 'A day to remember,' he said softly, and got into his car and waited until she had gone through the door and closed it behind her.

She wouldn't see him again, she supposed sadly, getting ready for bed.

She was quite right; there was neither sight nor sound of him for the next week. She did her best to forget him, quite unsuccessfully, and when Dr Douglas invited her to have dinner with him in Oban's leading restaurant she accepted, wearing one of her pretty new dresses, and listening with every sign of interest to his plans for the future. She gathered that they included her, but only vaguely; what was important to him was his career. He was ambitious, and she had the lowering feeling that it wouldn't much matter who he married as long as she fitted into his own plans.

Rosie thanked him prettily for her dinner, aware that she had no interest in him at all and, although he showed a flattering interest in her for the moment, it could be easily diverted. All the same it would do no harm to let Fergus assume that she had serious intentions of marrying Ian, even though it was very likely that he hadn't given her another thought.

She was wrong. Sir Fergus, engrossed in his work as he was, still had time to think about her—something which he did frequently. He had been in Edinburgh for more than a week when he had occasion to go to Oban to give his opinion upon a particularly complicated compound fracture of tibia and fibula. The leg had been crushed by a falling wall, and its fragmented bones would need assembling, wiring and rearranging into something resembling their original pattern, something at which he excelled. He spent a long morning at the hospital doing just that, assisted by the resident surgeon and watched by Ian Douglas.

Afterwards they had coffee in Sister's office, and the RSO had gone off to check the patient's condition, leaving Ian and Sir Fergus finishing their coffee.

The younger man was full of admiration. 'I mean to make my mark too,' he told Sir Fergus. 'General surgery. Only, of course I must get to Edinburgh first—there's no future for me here.'

Arrogant young pup, thought Sir Fergus, and wondered what Rosie, of all people, saw in him.

'I shouldn't be in too much of a hurry,' he advised quietly. 'A few years here will establish you. You plan to marry?'

'Marry? Certainly not. Perhaps in five or six years. A wife would be a millstone round my neck right now.

He laughed rather awkwardly because Sir Fergus was looking at him rather strangely.

'Popular local rumour has Rosie Macdonald as your future wife,' he observed blandly.

'Rosie? Good lord, no. She's a nice girl—we're friendly, but that's all. I fancy small fragile women who don't argue.'

Sir Fergus looked amused. 'Does Rosie argue?'

'All the time.' He added hastily, 'Mind you, sir, she's a charming girl.' He laughed a little. 'But I've no intention of settling down yet awhile.'

'A wise decision.' Sir Fergus got up. 'I must be off. Let me know how that leg does, will you? I'll be over in a day or so to check X-rays—get some more taken in a couple of days, will you?'

He didn't drive straight back to Edinburgh. He went to Inverard and found Rosie in the rose garden, trying to bring order to the tangled bushes, and attacking the weeds choking them. She had prudently worn an old dress and worn-out gym shoes she had found in the garden shed, and a pair of gardening-gloves sizes too large. She had gathered up her hair and tied it in an untidy tangle with a piece of twine, and her face shone with her exertions.

Sir Fergus, coming upon her silently, thought that she looked enchanting.

His 'Hello, Rosie' was uttered softly, but it surprised her none the less. She had been thinking about him too, and the bright colour flooded her face as she turned round.

'Oh, hello. Are you on your way home?'

'Yes.' He didn't say which home; he was, in fact, on his way back to Edinburgh and his house there. 'How are you, Rosie?'

'Me? Very well—and happy. There's such a lot to do, you know, the days aren't long enough.'

'No fun at all?' he asked with casual amusement. 'No friends, no young men?'

'Oh, well, yes—lots of friends...'

'And young Douglas, of course.'

'Yes, yes.'

She bent to tug at a recalcitrant weed, and she didn't look at him as she added, 'We see quite a lot of each other.'

'Naturally,' said Sir Fergus smoothly. 'Have you fixed the wedding day yet?'

The weed came away suddenly so that she almost lost her balance. Sir Fergus caught her neatly and set her upright.

'September would be a good month for a wedding,' he prompted, his eyes half closed so as to conceal their wicked gleam.

'Well, yes, but of course Ian is busy—it's a large practice, you know. We—that is, I, haven't decided.'

'Very wise,' said her companion gravely. 'When is your aunt marrying?'

'The day after tomorrow.'

'So you will be staying with your grandmother?'

'Yes. Mother is coming too—Father has too much to do; besides, men don't really like weddings, do they?'

'Er—possibly they find some pleasure in their own.'

She pushed back the dark curls. 'Would you like coffee? Mother will be delighted...'

'I've already been to the house, and your mother gave me coffee. I couldn't go without saying hello.'

Rosie took a grubby hand out of its glove. 'Please remember me to your mother; it was nice seeing you.'

She offered the hand, rather red in the face because last time he had kissed her and she wanted him to kiss her now.

He didn't. He shook her hand and smiled a little, and said, 'We'll meet again some time, I dare say, Rosie,' and he had gone before she could utter a suitable reply.

When she went into the house her mother said, 'Fergus called; did he find you?'

'Yes.' She didn't want to talk about him. 'Those rose beds are in a terrible mess, Mother—it will take a couple of years to get them back to what they were.'

'Yes, dear,' agreed Mrs Macdonald, and took care not to mention Fergus again.

The pair of them left for Edinburgh the following after-noon, and arrived at old Mrs Macdonald's house to find that lady giving orders right and left, deploring the fact that she had such a heartless daughter, and wanting to know where the rather splendid hat she had worn to her son's wedding some twenty ago could be. Rosie found the hat, a masterpiece of black straw, tulle and curled feathers, soothed her grandparent, helped get supper on the table, and retired to bed to lie awake wishing she was the bride and not the bridesmaid. A different bride-groom, of course, she reminded herself as she nodded off—Fergus, free from his shadowy fiancée and in love with her.

CHAPTER EIGHT

ROSIE was up early; much as her grandmother decried Aunt Carrie's wedding, old Mrs Macdonald intended to grace the ceremony in splendour. It took the combined efforts of Elspeth, her mother and herself to dress the old lady to her satisfaction, which gave them little time to get into their wedding finery. Old Mrs Macdonald left first with Elspeth in the hired car, and Rosie, by no means pleased with her appearance, since she had dressed in a great hurry, urged her mother into the car and drove across the city to Tron Church, anxious to get there before the bride.

She had a thankful ten minutes before Aunt Carrie was due to arrive; she saw her mother into a pew at the front of the church, already surprisingly full, and retreated to the porch where she smoothed down the soft silk of her simple dress, made sure that the wreath of flowers was firmly anchored on her curls, and sat down to wait.

Aunt Carrie was a little late—only to be expected—and in a flutter. She had chosen to wear a soft blue two-piece and a charming hat she would never have dared to wear while she had been living with old Mrs Macdonald, and Rosie was quick to tell her how pretty she looked.

'Oh, well, yes,' said Aunt Carrie, more disjointedly than ever. 'Is it all...? That is, it's too hot. Should I have worn...? I'm not sure...'

'You look smashing,' Rosie assured her lovingly. 'Here, carry your flowers—they go beautifully with your dress. Are you ready?'

Dr MacLeod was giving Aunt Carrie away; they walked up the aisle with Rosie behind them. The unexpected sight of Sir Fergus, towering over the other guests in one of the pews, caused her to falter in her slow pacing, but only for a moment. She went past him, looking ahead of her, apparently lost in the solemnity of the occasion.

The service was simple and short; they were walking down the aisle and out of the church in no time at all, followed by family and friends.

Rosie watched the elderly best man usher the happy couple into their car, and waited for him to accompany her in the first of the cars lined up. He joined her presently, looking harassed. 'I'd better get your family away first,' he told her worriedly.

'I'll drive Rosie back.' Sir Fergus's voice sounded to the bothered man like that of an old trusted friend; indeed, he knew Sir Fergus by sight.

'So kind,' he said hurriedly. 'There are several ladies, you understand.'

'Oh, I do indeed,' acknowledged Sir Fergus with what Rosie considered to be unnecessarily fulsome sympathy. 'Do go ahead and see to them.'

He hardly waited for the best man's thanks, but whisked Rosie away to the Rolls, and popped her into the front seat.

'Why are you here?' she asked.

He got into the car beside her. 'Your aunt invited me. She made a charming bride, did she not?' He turned to look at her. 'And you are a quite beautiful bridesmaid, Rosie.'

She mumbled something, feeling shy and then peevishly furious when he added, 'A rehearsal for being the bride yourself, perhaps?'

'Certainly not!' Her voice was frosty. 'Aren't you supposed to be looking after your patients?'

'Not until this afternoon. They're off just after one o'clock, aren't they? Leaving everyone feeling flat. Would you like to come to the Royal Infirmary with me and look around while I do some work?'

'Oh, may I? I would very much like to. Are you coming to the reception? It's only drinks and canapés. What time shall I come, and where do I go?'

'As soon as we've seen the happy pair off I'll drive you to your grandmother's house—that's where you are staying, isn't it?—you can have ten minutes to change. I'll hand you over to someone who will show you everything you might like to see.'

'Just like that? Don't you even have to ask someone?'

His firm mouth twitched. 'Well, no. I don't think that will be necessary.'

'Not even the matron?'

'Not even the matron. Here we are. Are there to be many guests?'

'No, just family and William Brodie's friends and an odd cousin or two of his.'

He parked the car, and they went into the hotel and were at once separated—she to be the centre of the vague cousins' attention, he to confer gravely with her grandmother, looking, it must be admitted, rather like the bad fairy bent on casting gloom over the party. Not that she was given the chance; Sir Fergus, used to dealing with awkward patients, diverted the old lady's attention away from Carrie's happy face, and listened with becoming gravity to a detailed description of old Mrs Macdonald's fragile state before reassuring her with such a positive manner that she actually accepted a second glass of champagne.

The last of the confetti had barely been thrown when Sir Fergus was at Rosie's elbow. 'Come on, I've spoken to your mother.'

Rosie found her mother talking to Dr MacLeod. 'Mother,' she began, to be interrupted by her mother's,

'Have a lovely time, darling. Dr MacLeod will drive Granny and me back. Don't keep Fergus waiting.'

Outside her grandmother's house he got out to help her. 'Ten minutes,' he reminded her, and as she jumped out and hurried into the house he got back into the car.

She managed it in nine minutes, darting through the door looking as fresh as a daisy in a pretty cotton dress and a little jacket, her hair neatly brushed, her feet thrust into low-heeled sandals with an eye to the hospital corridors she supposed she would traipse up and down later on.

'What time do you have to be at the hospital?' she asked as he stowed her back into the car.

'I have a list for quarter-past two,' he told her.

'Oh, plenty of time...'

'Yes.' He turned the car and drove away in the opposite direction to which she had expected to go.

'The infirmary is over there, isn't it?' She waved an arm in its general direction.

'Yes, but I live in Moray Place. We will have lunch first. I cannot and will not operate with hollow insides.'

Not true, of course; many a time he had, in an emergency, got out of his bed to operate in the small hours and well into the day without so much as a cup of tea. He certainly didn't stop for a meal if it happened to infringe upon his surgery. His theatre sister swallowed whatever she had time for between cases, and sent her long-suffering nurses to their dinners while the theatre was prepared for the next case, with him standing there like a patient giant.

It was but a short distance to Moray Place. It looked solid and elegant in the early-afternoon sun, and tall houses beautifully maintained, the garden in its centre bright with shrubs and flowers. Sir Fergus stopped before such a house at the end of the semi-circular terrace, and got out.

'Mrs Meikle will have everything ready,' he observed as he opened Rosie's door and swept her across the pavement, and indeed that lady had the door open before they reached it. Sir Fergus paused long enough to make introductions.

'Twenty minutes, Mrs Meikle, if you can manage that; we need to be away not a minute later than that.'

'Bless you, Mr Fergus, everything's waiting to be popped into your mouths.'

He threw an arm around her plump shoulders. 'Good, we'll go straight into the dining-room.'

He opened a door in the narrow hall, and ushered Rosie inside. The room was at the back of the house overlooking a pleasant garden, its doors open on to a terrace. Gyp came prancing in, delighted to see them, and Sir Fergus said, 'Would you like a drink? Sherry?'

The champagne Rosie had had after the wedding was still giving her an agreeably fizzy feeling. 'No, thank you.'

He pulled out a chair at the circular table, its cloth snowy-white, the silver gleaming on it, the crystal sparkling.

'Tonic water? Lemonade? Mrs Meikle makes her own.'

A sturdy girl came in with watercress soup, very cold and with a dash of cream in it, and a basket of rolls, and Rosie who had managed to nibble only a handful of the canapés with the champagne, fell to with unself-conscious pleasure, watched appreciatively by her companion.

The soup was followed by hot cheese puffs and a green salad, and finally coffee, taken in an atmosphere which gave no indication of haste; indeed, Sir Fergus carried on a rambling conversation without looking at the clock once. Nevertheless, they left the house within the half-hour, and when they reached the hospital it still wanted ten minutes to a quarter-past the hour.

Rosie was whisked through the entrance hall and into a lift before she had the time to look around her, walked briskly down a number of corridors, up and down a staircase or two, and was handed over to a fierce-looking middle-aged lady, upholstered in dark blue, and wearing a very starched cap on her iron-grey hair.

The professor flung an arm round her. 'Becky, dear, here is Rosie, just as I promised. Allow her to poke her nose into whatever interests her, will you? And if I'm not finished by four o'clock or thereabouts sit her down with a good book until I am.'

To Rosie's astonishment he gave the elderly shoulders a friendly hug, and received a warm smile in return.

'Rosie, this is Sister Wallace. She used to be my theatre sister, now she is the Theatre Superintendent and only scrubs for me on special occasions. She will take you round the hospital and tell you anything you want to know.'

He gave her a brisk nod and stalked away, and Sister Wallace said, 'Well, shall we have a cup of tea before we start? There's a lot to see.' She turned a bright, enquiring eye on Rosie, 'You're a lucky girl, the professor's doing you a great favour.'

Rosie murmured suitably, and they repaired to Sister's office, where they drank tea and exchanged small talk until there was no more tea left in the pot.

'Now where shall it be first? The maternity pavilion? The eye pavilion? Outpatients?'

Rosie put down her cup. 'I'd like to see where Sir Fergus works, please.'

Sister Wallace's beady eyes studied Rosie thoughtfully. 'Why not? You cannot go into Theatre, of course, but you may look through the portholes, and if you are not squeamish you may observe him operating from the gallery.'

The porthole revealed the anaesthetic room, a patient on a trolley and, presumably, the anaesthetist. 'The patient has had a pre-med,' explained Sister Wallace, 'which relaxes him sufficiently to make him composed.'

Then she led the way along a corridor, and opened a door which gave on to a gallery already almost filled with white-coated students.

'You are sure that you wish to watch? I can't have you fainting here.'

'I shan't faint, although I don't suppose I shall want to stay for long.'

The patient was on the table surrounded by shrouded figures, and it was very quiet. Sir Fergus, gowned and gloved, came into view, and his 'Good afternoon, Sister,' uttered in an unhurried and casual voice, made the surroundings perfectly normal, so that Rosie, peering down and wondering if she should be there after all, felt reassured.

Sir Fergus murmured something to the theatre sister, put out a gloved hand and was handed a scalpel, and Rosie very sensibly closed her eyes.

When she opened them cautiously his vast back obscured her view, which was just as well, and when Sister Wallace plucked at her arm she went willingly enough back to the corridor.

'I just wanted to know,' she explained to her companion. 'I mean, I knew he was a surgeon, but I could only imagine... Does he ever make a mistake?'

Sister Wallace allowed herself a chuckle. 'No! Would you like to see his wards?'

'Yes, please.'

The afternoon flew by; Rosie, led from one end of the hospital to the other, was enthralled. She poked her pretty head into every corner she was permitted, asking endless questions which Sister Wallace answered patiently, if briefly, until at last she was led back to that lady's office and told to sit down while a tray of tea was brought.

With it came Sir Fergus, looking the epitome of the well-dressed gentleman who wouldn't know a scalpel if he saw one.

'You look different,' remarked Rosie.

'Er—in what way?' he wanted to know.

'Well, I suppose it's the clothes; you looked so—so as though everyone in the theatre would do what you told them to do without asking why.'

He took the tea Sister Wallace handed to him.

'I should jolly well hope so, or the place would be bedlam!'

Sister Wallace allowed herself a chuckle. 'We were in the gallery.'

'Only I closed my eyes when you took that knife,' Rosie said, and then, 'When I opened them again I could only see your back.' She bit into the *petit beurre* biscuit she had been offered. 'Are you going to operate again or have you finished for today?'

He glanced at his watch. 'Outpatients in half an hour, and then a quick check-up of today's cases.'

'Not to mention a couple of private patients this evening and letters to dictate,' added Sister Wallace drily.

'Then I'll go now. Thank you for letting me see round the Infirmary, I really was interested,' Rosie said enthusiastically.

She got to her feet, shook Sister Wallace's hand, offered a hand to Sir Fergus, and made for the door. He was there before her.

'I'll drive you back,'

He sounded like a man with nothing to do for the rest of the day.

'A breath of fresh air will be welcome.' He looked over his shoulder at Sister Wallace. 'Thanks, Becky, let them know in OPD, will you?'

Rosie, a calm girl, found that calm shattered.

'I can go back on my own,' she pointed out as they started their devious journey back to the entrance. She might just as well have been addressing the air, for Sir Fergus took no notice of her.

She tried again. 'There is no need...' This also was ignored; instead she was swept out to the Rolls, shoved into the front seat with surprisingly gentle hands, and driven back, through the Grassmarket, past the library, down the Mound, into Princes Street, and so eventually to her grandmother's house.

Rosie had sat silent, but now she said, 'Will you come in? I'm sure Granny will be pleased to see you.'

He was already getting out of the car, and had opened her door before he replied, 'No time.' He bent and kissed her swiftly, and got back into the car and drove away.

Rosie glanced at her watch; Sister Wallace had told her that he was a stickler for punctuality. He was going to have to drive very fast...

She went indoors to find her mother in the drawing-room with a tea-tray before her. 'Your Granny is tired, she's having a cup of tea in her room, she said. Sit down, darling, and have a cup with me. Did you have an interesting afternoon?'

'Very. I went everywhere with the theatre superintendent.'

'You didn't see Fergus?' Mrs Macdonald's voice was indifferent.

'Oh, yes. I watched him operate, but only for a minute or two, and then I didn't look... He brought me back.'

'He didn't want to come in?'

'He has an Outpatients clinic this afternoon.'

'Oh, well, perhaps he will find time to pay us a visit before we go back.' Mrs Macdonald cast a look at her daughter's downcast face. 'I thought we might go home in a couple of days—there's no hurry.'

Anything could happen in a couple of days, thought Rosie, allowing herself a pleasant daydream.

The daydream was shattered that evening.

Rosie and her mother, intent on an evening stroll, were standing on the pavement making up their minds which way to walk when the Rolls went by. Sir Fergus was driving, and sitting beside him was the same girl who she had seen before. What was more, he saw them standing there, and lifted a hand in greeting.

'What a pretty girl,' observed Mrs Macdonald. 'Do you suppose she's the one he's going to marry?'

'I've no idea,' said Rosie waspishly, 'and I'm not really interested.'

She marched her parent in the opposite direction to that in which the Rolls had been driven. 'The wedding went off very nicely, didn't it? I'm sure they'll be very happy.'

'They will. I thought your aunt looked charming. What would you like to do tomorrow, Rosie?'

'Go home.' And, at her mother's surprised look she added, 'Well, there's nothing to do in Edinburgh, and Granny is very snappish. That is, unless you want to do some shopping, Mother?'

Mrs Macdonald, who had been looking forward to a pleasant browse down Princes Street and possibly the purchase of some inexpensive garment which wouldn't make her feel too much of a spendthrift, replied promptly, realising that Rosie's sudden urge to get away from Edinburgh had been uttered in urgent tones not to be ignored.

'Shopping? No, dear—I thought I'd come again in the autumn, when I'll need a new coat. There's nothing I want...'

A brave lie, but she was rewarded by the relief on Rosie's face, and she wondered what had happened to make Rosie—a girl with a normal interest in fashion—turn her back on the delights of the Edinburgh shops. Something to do with Fergus? But he had always treated Rosie with a casual friendliness now that they had decided to like each other after all; besides, had she not said on several occasions that he was thinking of getting married? Perhaps it was that girl sitting beside him in the car.

Old Mrs Macdonald, still brooding darkly over Aunt Carrie and, when she wasn't doing that, criticising the wedding, expressed the opinion, when it was suggested that Rosie and her mother should return home the very next day, that she would prefer their room to their company.

'I am an old woman, alone and defenceless, abandoned by all but my faithful maid. Go home, do!'

These piteous words were uttered in a bad-tempered and very loud voice which rather spoilt their effect, especially when she added, 'In any case you would have had to leave on the day after tomorrow; I have arranged one of my bridge parties, and since neither of you have the least idea how to play with intelligence I had no intention of asking you to make up a four.'

'Well, now, isn't that fortunate,' observed her daughter-in-law mildly, avoiding Rosie's eye. 'If we leave after breakfast that will give you plenty of time to arrange things.'

'Will Elspeth be able to cope on her own?' asked Rosie.

'I have engaged a very good daily woman, which will allow Elspeth more time in which to look after me. I must say, Rosie, that she gives me more care and attention than my own kith and kin. I was bitterly disappointed at your lack of concern when I sprained my ankle, and the subsequent agony I endured.'

Rosie got up from her chair. 'Dear Granny,' she said cheerfully, and dropped a kiss on the beautifully dressed, still dark hair. 'I shall go and pack our things so that we can leave directly after breakfast. Goodnight.'

She dropped a kiss on her mother's cheek as she passed her chair. 'Goodnight, Mother, don't stay up too late.'

They left after breakfast after a severe scolding from old Mrs Macdonald, and Rosie drove thankfully through the city and took the road home, taking care not to look around her too much in case she should see Fergus in the Rolls. There was no sign of him, though, and she wondered unhappily when she would see him again. Probably never, she reflected gloomily, her spirits at their lowest possible ebb.

It was great to be home again, to tell her father about the wedding, go round the garden to see what had grown in two days, to take Hobb for a walk, visit Meg's cottage because she wasn't sure if the youngest child's spots were measles or chicken pox, and consult Old Robert about the strawberry bed. Her day was filled with mundane tasks, and she was almost, but not quite, happy.

It was measles; the next morning Rosie phoned Dr Douglas, and when he arrived later and her mother had given him coffee she walked with him to Meg's cottage and swept the other children out of his way while Meg took him to see the small sufferer, and when he returned she offered to drive in to Oban and fetch the penicillin he had prescribed, since the child was feverish and chesty.

They walked back to his car, talking about this and that, when he gave a sudden laugh. 'You'll love this,' he declared. 'Professor Cameron was operating a week or so ago, and we got talking—about my future and so on. He actually thought that you and I were going to marry! I quickly put him right, I can tell you...I wonder who gave him that idea? Of all the nonsense...!'

Rosie swallowed rage. 'How frightfully funny,' she said, and actually achieved a laugh. 'As though I'd marry you, anyway...'

'I'm not such a bad catch,' he observed quickly.

'I'm sure you're not,' she observed sweetly, 'only not for me—you'll find some nice little thing. The professor must have been amused?'

'Funnily enough he didn't say much, and he's got such a poker-face one never knows if he's amused or angry, or just bored.'

'Probably bored. Do you intend to visit little Jamie again?'

'Will you let me know if his temperature goes down, say, in a couple of days? If it doesn't I'll come and take another look.' He got into his car, rolled down the window, and asked, 'I say, you're not peeved are you? About that nonsense about us?'

'Peeved? Of course not. Someone was enjoying a joke at our expense.' She gave him a brilliant smile. 'I'll phone you about little Jamie; goodbye.'

She watched him drive away, standing there seething. Fergus had mentioned Ian several times—had talked about them getting married, had asked if she had fixed the wedding day, and all the while he had known... She would never forgive him; better still she would take great care never to see him again. A resolve which cast her into a state of the deepest depression.

She saw him the very next day. She was in the attics, searching for a particular basket Simpkins had always slept in which had been banished to the attics along with a number of unwanted chairs and tables when her uncle had taken over, and the faint sounds of a car stopping below sent her to the tiny dormer windows. Sir Fergus was getting out in his unhurried fashion so that she had time to fly down the narrow wooden back stairs which opened into the kitchen, and nip through the kitchen door before he had so much as gained the front hall.

She encountered Old Robert at the far end of the kitchen garden, bending over his row of winter cabbages. 'Don't tell anyone you've seen me,' she begged as she went past him, and ran smartly through the little door in the high brick wall which separated the garden from the small paddock beyond it. Beyond that was the river, tumbling over the rocks with the stepping-stones to its further bank. Rosie nipped over them with the ease of familiarity, and started making her way towards the line of fir trees at the foot of the hills ahead of her. She was out of earshot now and, unless anyone was looking that way, out of sight too.

She slowed down, and presently sat down on a dead tree-trunk to think, something she hadn't done since the moment when she had seen Fergus getting out of the Rolls. It had been silly to run away, she realised now; sooner or later she was bound to meet him. All the same, she had no intention of going back to the house.

The sun, hidden behind a cloud, shone with sudden brilliance, and Sir Fergus, standing at the drawing-room window talking to her mother, had a momentary and clear view of her.

'She was in the attics,' Mrs Macdonald was saying. 'Why, she must have been there still when you drove up, for I was in the bedroom below and I could hear her dragging something along the floor. The floors need repairing, you know.'

Sir Fergus made a pleasant rejoinder, and added, 'She is on the other side of the river, sitting on a tree stump. I'll stroll over...'

Rosie's attention had been taken by a squirrel near by, and she had turned away from the house and the river. Sir Fergus, despite his size and bulk, could move silently when he wished to do so, and he was beside her before she was aware of it, a firm, gentle hand on her shoulder as she started up.

'Now why should you run away?' he wanted to know.

'Run away? What makes you think that? I felt like taking a stroll...'

A remark he ignored. 'Why did you tell me that you and young Douglas were going to marry? And why——?'

'Questions, questions,' cut in Rosie peevishly. 'I shan't tell you.'

'Then I'll answer them for you,' said Sir Fergus, studying her flushed face.

'Don't you dare! I'll never speak to you again. I wasn't going to, anyway.'

'Now I wonder why? What have I done or not done, or said or not said?'

He sounded as though he was trying not to laugh.

'Nothing, absolutely nothing. Why are you making such a fuss? And why aren't you in Edinburgh at the hospital?'

'I came here to see you, but you don't want to see me, do you, Rosie?'

'No I don't. I do long for you to go away...'

He stood up. 'Very well, Rosie.' He sounded offhand, as though it didn't matter in the least. 'What a perfectly splendid morning, isn't it? I could wish I were a hill-shepherd or a farmer.'

He smiled into her upturned, surprised face, and went away without another word. She stared after him until he had crossed the river and gone through the little door, and presently, silently sitting there, relieved her feelings by a good cry.

She had been silly and childish; she owned up to that, but what did that matter? He was going to marry soon; all he wanted from her was a casual friendship, and that, from her point of view, would be impossible. All the same, if she had answered him light-heartedly, treated the whole thing as a joke, they could have parted with polite, even if insincere, hopes to meet at some time, and in time their friendship would have died a natural death. Oh, well, it was too late now.

She went back to the house, back to the attics, where she banged and thumped around discarded furniture, old trunks and piles of books, making a great deal of noise, so that by lunchtime she was sufficiently restored to express the opinion that it was surprising Sir Fergus had called that morning.

'He only stayed for a few minutes,' she was at pains to explain. 'Had he been in Oban? He didn't say...'

'On his way home, I dare say,' said her father, and asked who was taking her to the Highland Ball at Fort William the following week.

'Ian Douglas. It should be fun.' It proved a topic of conversation for the rest of the meal.

She went to see Jamie the next day. He was pretty spotty and still feverish; Ian Douglas had said that there was no need to phone him for a couple of days, but she had her own reasons for ringing him. She reported on Jamie, and then said, 'Ian, will you do me a favour?'

'Of course—that is, if I can.'

'Are you going to the ball at Fort William? You are? Alone? Good, will you take me? You don't need to stay with me the whole evening, I just want someone to go with.'

'Love to—didn't ask before; I thought Sir Fergus might be going, he usually does.'

Rosie was aware of that; of course he would be there. His estate was close by, and his family was well-known in Cameron country.

'Will you call for me? Come to dinner if you like.'

'Delighted. Eight o'clock?'

She went away to tell her mother, who said, 'How nice, dear,' and began to plan the menu while she wondered just what had gone wrong between Rosie and Fergus to make her so very cheerful and chatty and he, when he had left on the previous morning, so politely inscrutable. Perhaps they would see each other at the ball and make it up.

Ian Douglas, arriving for dinner on the night of the ball, had to admit that Rosie, in white chiffon and her tartan sash, was certainly one of the prettiest girls he had met. In five years' time, he mused, she might be

just the wife I'll be looking for. Not much money, but
good family, and a splendid figure as well as beautiful.
A pity she argues...!

She didn't argue over dinner, however; she was the
soul of amiability. He got into the car beside her presently, pleased at the prospect of a delightful evening
ahead of him.

Inverlochy Castle Hotel was a grey stone pile with Ben
Nevis in the background, a fitting background for the
guests, the women in their white dresses and tartan, the
men in dress kilts and here and there a white tie. The
dancing was well under way when they arrived, and they
joined in almost at once. Rosie was a good dancer, and
the reels were as much to her liking as the more con-
ventional dances. Ian was a good partner, too, and since
both of them knew a number of people there they parted
from time to time until they met for the supper.

They shared a table with half a dozen friends, and it
was as they were making their way to it that Rosie saw
Sir Fergus. She went rather pale at the sight of him,
magnificent in his kilt, talking to the Provost's eldest
daughter—a girl Rosie had never liked, and now heartily
and instantly hated. If she could have avoided him she
would have done so, but there was no way of doing that,
so she gave him a glittering smile and a glare which would
have shaken a lesser man, paused long enough to go into
raptures over his companion's dress, and sailed on, to
become the life and soul of the party at her table.

She danced every dance after supper, her strong
feelings giving her a splendid colour and sparkling eyes
while she hoped in vain that Fergus would ask her to
dance so that she might refuse him. As far as he was
concerned she might not have been there.

She couldn't avoid him altogether, though. The
dancing over and 'Auld Lang Syne' sung, everyone was
milling around in the hotel foyer, finding coats, having
a last minute chat, calling goodnights. Ian had gone to
get his car, and Rosie stood, wrapped in her mother's
rather grand velvet cloak, exchanging goodbyes with
those she knew. There had been no sign of Sir Fergus;
probably, she thought sourly, he was taking the
Provost's daughter home. She scowled at the very idea,
and then jumped as he bent to say in her ear,

'A delightful evening, was it not, Rosie? Young
Douglas must feel very proud of you.'

She smiled brightly at an old friend of her mother's,
and waved to a girl with whom she had been at school
before she replied.

'You have no need to poke fun,' she told him bitterly.
'It must have amused you very much when Ian told you
that—that——' She broke off to exchange a word with
old Sir William Bruce, eighty if he was a day, and who
had never been known to miss a ball. Then she turned
a glittering eye upon Sir Fergus, towering beside her.

'I hope I never see you again,' she asserted and, for
the benefit of two acquaintances who had paused close
by, she added sweetly, 'You must enjoy an evening out,
Sir Fergus; it must make a nice change from bones.'

Her smile was a delight.

'And here is Ian...'

She floated gracefully away to where Ian was standing.
No one watching her would have known that her desire
to turn round and fling herself into Sir Fergus's arms
was so strong that she felt quite faint...

CHAPTER NINE

IAN DOUGLAS had enjoyed himself, and he said so at some length as he drove away from Fort William.

'That girl the professor was dancing with,' he enthused, 'the Provost's daughter, isn't she? A pretty creature, and very gentle, wasn't she? They made a handsome couple—I must say Sir Fergus looks his best in a kilt.'

Rosie agreed through gritted teeth. The evening hadn't gone according to plan; if he had been there at the moment and she had been capable of it she would have done Sir Fergus an injury. Mere wishful thinking, of course; he was as solid as an oak, and although she was a well-built girl she would have made no impression on him unless she had had a hammer handy. She wished she had a hammer, and brooded upon this prospect for some time while Ian waffled on about the provost's daughter.

At Inverard she invited him in for coffee, and was thankful when he refused. It was past two o'clock by now, and she wanted above all things to get to her bed and sleep. She bade him goodnight and thanked him prettily for being her escort, saw him on his way, and went thankfully to her room. She had been longing for her bed, but now that she was in it at last she was wide awake, her head full of Sir Fergus, who, none the less, she never wanted to see again. She slept at last and, inevitably, dreamed of him.

She woke at her usual time, and at breakfast gave her parents a lively account of the ball, passing on the messages she had been given by their friends, detailing at length the various dresses, the excellent band and the splendid buffet-supper; from the sound of it she had had the time of her life, but her pale face and the pinkened tip of her beautiful nose gave that the lie.

Her mother gave her a thoughtful glance. 'Was Fergus there?' she asked.

'Fergus? Oh, yes—he was with the Provost's party, but there was such a crush we hardly spoke...'

'He must look fine in the kilt?'

'Yes, yes he does.' Rosie crumbled a slice of toast.

'I thought it might be a good idea if I phone round to get the knitters organised. I was talking to Lady MacTavish, and she was telling me that there's a new boutique opening in Inverness, planning to sell hand-knitted goods. I thought I might find out a bit more about it.'

If this abrupt change in the conversation surprised Mrs Macdonald she didn't comment upon it, but discussed the knitting question at some length, and then suggested that Rosie might like to find Old Robert and ask him to dig some potatoes. Something Rosie not only did, but also helped him dig them, and the effort needed helped her to forget the feeling of desolation which was threatening to swamp her.

Just for a few days she nurtured the hope that Sir Fergus might come to Inverard, which she had to admit was silly, for he had no reason to do so, and she cried quietly into her pillow each night.

Which was a pity for, in actual fact visiting her was the one thing the professor wished to do more than anything else. He was quite sure about that, but he wasn't quite sure about Rosie; he loved her and he was in love with her and he had every intention of marrying her, but only when she was ready and willing. He wasn't a conceited man, but he was aware that if he exerted his charm and will she could be plucked like an apple from a tree. He didn't want that; he wanted her to fall, as it were, of her own accord into his waiting hand.

So the days went by, and Rosie busied herself getting her knitters organised for the winter. Many of them lived in isolated glens, and depended upon her to bring wool and patterns and collect their work when it was finished; she got them organised, for there had been no one else to do it while her uncle had lived at Inverard, and then she took herself off to Inverness to seek out the owner of the boutique there.

The owners were more than willing to take anything she could bring them; the samples she had brought with her were right for the tourist market, and they would pay well. She left the shop feeling satisfied, and came face to face with Mrs Cameron.

'My dear, what a delightful surprise! And just when I was wondering if I should stop for a cup of coffee. Let us pop into this café, I shall be glad to rest for a little while.'

The meeting was unexpected; besides, Mrs Cameron had a compelling manner. Rosie found herself sitting at a small table exchanging small talk.

'You really must pay me another visit, Rosie,' said Mrs Cameron. 'Fergus told me that you had been at the ball, but I know these affairs are crowded—no chance to talk.'

She prattled on, seemingly unaware of Rosie's replies, while she studied the pretty face opposite her. Fergus had been remarkably terse whenever she had mentioned Rosie; what was more, he was working harder than ever and, when he did go to his home, walked miles with the dogs. Something wasn't quite right, but he was a patient man, and she had no doubt that he would get whatever he wanted—and she was sure that it was Rosie—in his own good time. She wondered if they had quarrelled, and thought it unlikely. A misunderstanding, perhaps?

She sighed; when one was in love one was so sensitive.

They talked about the knitting for some time, and she observed, 'I don't come to Inverness very often, do you, Rosie? But it was an opportunity I couldn't miss today. Fergus is operating at the Northern Infirmary, and I needed some odds and ends. He will meet me for lunch. I suppose you wouldn't care to join us?'

Rosie had gone pale at the very idea. 'I—well, I'm afraid I have to get back.'

She sought feverishly for an excuse, watched with some interest by Mrs Cameron.

'It's very kind of you, I would have enjoyed it very much, but I promised to let Mrs Barr know about this knitting—she really runs it once it's organised, you see. I just take round the wool and collect it.'

She stopped, aware that she was babbling, and Mrs Cameron, a kind woman, said soothingly, 'What a pity—but I quite see that you can't stop. It's quite a long drive back, isn't it? It's been delightful seeing you again; I shall write and arrange a day for you to come over to lunch, and do bring your mother with you.'

They parted outside the café, and Rosie went back to the car park and got into the car, and drove out of

Inverness absurdly afraid that she was going to bump into Fergus too if she stayed there a moment longer.

When he went into the foyer of the station hotel his mother was already there. He didn't see her at once, and she was able to study him unobserved. He looked tired, and she wasn't surprised at that, but he looked inscrutable too. A bad sign. He saw her, and came over to her table and sat down.

She smiled and said, 'I had coffee with Rosie...'

She was right, she knew she was. His face became a bland mask. He lifted a finger to a waiter, and said quietly, 'Oh? Rather far from home, surely?'

'She is getting the cottage industry going again—knitting and so forth. Had to come here to get orders from a boutique. I asked her to have lunch with us, but she had to hurry back. Such a pretty girl, but she looked tired—or do I mean unhappy?'

She cast a quick look at her son, and went on quickly, 'Have you had a very busy morning? What time will you be finished, dear? I still have quite a lot of shopping...'

'I've several patients to see, but I should be through by half-past four or thereabouts. Will you be all right until then?'

'Of course, dear. I shall treat myself to tea at that chic little place where they have those delicious chocolate cakes.'

Several days later Rosie drove to Fort William to have lunch with Lady MacTavish and tell her that she had been successful with the boutique at Inverness. Lunch was a leisurely meal and, by the time her hostess had asked her advice about the new material she had just bought for curtains, and taken her up to the attics to search for a particular piece of tapestry she had found there and mislaid, it was time for tea. After tea the daughter of the house and her husband arrived, and since she and Rosie hadn't seen each other since Rosie had gone to England the time flew by.

'You must stay for supper,' insisted Lady MacTavish. 'I'll give your mother a ring, dear. We have seen so little of you, and I want to know about Wiltshire, and you and Chloe have such a lot to talk about still.'

So Rosie stayed, and by the time she had made her farewells the evening was well advanced and the sky had clouded over.

It started to rain within a few minutes of leaving Fort William, and with the rain came great gusts of wind so that she had to slow down once she had left the town behind her. The mountains were shrouded in clouds, the whole wild countryside was obscured by the downpour, the road empty of traffic.

She drove on steadily; she knew the way like the back of her hand and the car was running well. She had passed Ballachulish and was driving along a lonely stretch of road skirting the Rannoch Moor when she caught a glimpse of a light well away from the road. She slowed the car and took a second look, and then stopped. There were no crofts there, no huts used for sheltering walkers, only bog and pools and wild ground.

The light was flickering on and off and moving around as though someone was waving a torch. The light was bad, but she thought it came from an outcrop of rock well away from the road, probably on the West Highland Way. The rain had settled down into a steady drizzle. She got out of the car, got her shower-jacket from the boot and put it on, wishing at the same time that she had put her wellies in as well. At least she had a powerful torch with her. She locked the car doors, checked the light once more, and set off across the moor. She knew the moor quite well, and the walk was about three miles away, she reckoned, although the light appeared to be much nearer than that. Probably someone had strayed from the walk and got lost. She struck out across the rough ground, first flashing her torch in reply to the wavering light in the distance, praying that they didn't switch off their own light.

It was further than she had thought; it took her twenty minutes to get within shouting distance of the light. Her 'hello' brought an answering cry and five minutes later she, slowly clambering over rough ground strewn with rock, almost fell over the torch-holder.

A young man, little more than a boy, lying awkwardly in a patch of bog, very wet, with a leg twisted under him and blood matting his hair.

She dropped down beside him, took off her jacket, and slipped it carefully under his head.

'How long?' she asked. 'And where does it hurt? I'll try and make you more comfortable.'

Brave words, for she guessed that the leg was broken, but at least she could help him out of the bog.

His voice was faint. 'I lost my way. Caught my foot on a rock or something and fell over backwards, hit my head...'

'Your leg hurts?'

'No. Can't feel anything.' His anxious eyes sought hers. 'It's broken isn't it? So why can't I feel it?'

Rosie said bracingly, 'I dare say you're numb with cold. Does your head ache?'

'Yes.'

He was mumbling now, and she had to bend low to hear him.

'Did it for a dare...' And then, 'Don't leave me alone...'

'Of course not. I've got a powerful torch with me, any car passing will see it. Try and go to sleep for a while. I promise you I won't go away.'

He closed his eyes, and she squatted down beside him. He felt very cold, and he was wet to his skin, too, but then so was she. She flashed the light and then she switched it off—better to save it until she saw the headlights of a car on the distant road.

'Someone will be along presently,' she said cheerfully, and turned a cautious light on to his face. He didn't answer. He appeared to be asleep, but his breathing was loud and snoring, and his eyes weren't quite closed. A *frisson* of fear shot through her. She didn't dare to move him; he had said that he couldn't feel his legs—perhaps he had damaged his spine. On the other hand, they couldn't stay there.

But they might have to, she reminded herself—at least until morning, when there was a chance that someone might see them.

It was still raining and very windy. The clouds hung low over the mountains around them, and it was no longer possible to see any distance. Rosie doubted if anyone from the road would see her torch, and even if they did they might not stop. It was time to get help.

'Oh, God,' whispered Rosie, 'do please send Fergus.' She meant every word of it, and she felt better having said it. Her voice was quite cheerful when she observed to the unconscious boy beside her, 'He'll be along presently; we just have to be patient.'

It was after midnight as Fergus drove through Bridge of Orchy, past the hotel, now in darkness, and on to the desolate stretch of road curving round the moor. He had had a long, hard day, and he was tired, and he was looking forward to a day at home. He wanted time to think, to decide what to do about Rosie. A patient man, his patience was fast running out. Perhaps he had been too patient...

He said to the sleeping Gyp, curled up beside him, 'I'll go and see her tomorrow.'

The road circled, and he caught the faint flash of a torch away to the right of the road. He slowed the car's speed and watched for it and, when it flashed again, drove on until he was level with it.

'We had better take a look,' he told Gyp, and got out of the car, and saw Rosie's car in the curve of the road ahead of him.

'No lights, the little fool,' he muttered, and went to take a look. There was no sign of damage or any kind of violence, and it was securely locked. She had left it deliberately, and for a good reason. He whistled to Gyp, switched on his torch, and flashed it in the direction of the tiny pin-point of light.

It flashed back at once, and he set off, as familiar with his surroundings as she had been, going steadily and, as he neared the light, whistling cheerfully. Her nerves would be stretched like violin strings, he guessed, and to creep upon her silently might send her into screaming hysterics.

Rosie was so cold and wet she was oblivious of anything else. Now and again she waved the torch, but it was a purely mechanical gesture, while her other hand clutched the cold hand of the boy beside her. Sir Fergus's rendering of 'O, my luve's like a red red rose...' roused her as nothing else would have done. She started to get to her feet, but she was stiff and numb with cold, and she was still scrabbling around when Gyp pushed up against her and licked her hand, waving a tail with the pleasure of meeting her again.

Sir Fergus paused when he saw her, taking in everything at a glance. The next moment he had swept her up gently and was holding her close, his great arms tightened around her.

'My brave little love,' he said softly, and bent to kiss her with a most satisfying urgency before setting her down on a nearby rock.

When he spoke he might have been in one of his hospital wards.

'How long? And has he been conscious at all?'

'It wasn't quite nine o'clock when I left the car; he was conscious then. I didn't move him because I think his leg is broken, but he said he couldn't feel anything.'

'Good girl.' He was squatting beside the boy, examining the inert body. 'And you're quite right, the leg is broken, and I suspect that his back is damaged. Any idea how it happened?'

She was still bewildered from his kiss. 'He was lost— he's been on the West Highland Way—on his own, for a dare. He fell over something and went over backwards. He—he stopped talking soon after I got here.'

Sir Fergus got to his feet. 'I'm going back to the car to phone for help. Gyp will stay with you.'

He took off his weatherproof jacket, took off the pullover he was wearing, and pulled it over her wet head, stuck her arms in the sleeves, and pulled it down over her sopping dress. He did it very gently and impersonally.

'Mustn't let you get cold,' he told her in a voice as impersonal as his manner, so that she decided that she had imagined his kiss.

'Will you be long?'

'It's about a mile to the road—I should be back within half an hour.'

She watched him go without a word. Only Gyp, told to 'stay', whimpered very softly as her master started to wend his way back to the road.

Once at the car he alerted the mountain rescue post a few miles away, warned the hospital at Fort William, asked for an ambulance and the police, and finally phoned Rosie's home.

'Mrs Macdonald, Rosie will be coming home rather late. There's been an accident—she's not involved, but she is waiting with the lad who's injured until we can get him to hospital. I'll see that she gets safely home.'

Mrs Macdonald kept her voice steady. 'We'll wait up, Fergus, and thank you for ringing—we were beginning to wonder. I won't keep you.'

He started back across the moor, desolate in the dark; the mountain rescue team would come presently, and then the others from Fort William. Getting the lad to the ambulance would be a slow job. It was difficult to be sure he was unconscious, but as well as a badly broken leg there was almost certainly a fractured spine.

Sir Fergus tramped along, already weighing the pros and cons of the situation, while at the back of his head he was conscious of Rosie's beautiful face and the expression on it when she had seen him. He allowed his thoughts to dwell on it for a moment with the deepest satisfaction.

A satisfaction which almost rocked him off his feet when he reached the bedraggled group among the rocks, for the face Rosie turned to him held a sudden glow of enormous happiness at the sight of him. But her words were prosaic enough.

'Will they be long? He is so cold; I've been rubbing his hands and arms.'

Sir Fergus crouched down beside the boy. 'About half an hour, I should think. We must keep him as warm as possible. Gyp...' The dog came to him at once and, obedient to his quiet command, lay down close to the lad.

'He's wet, but he's warm, too. Go on rubbing that arm, Rosie; I'm going to take a closer look.'

Rosie was tired and wet and still rather frightened, but she did as she was told, watching Sir Fergus carefully probing, knowing that there was really no need to be frightened now that he was there beside her in complete command of the situation, knowing what to do, and doing it with calm assurance. She rubbed the flaccid arm until her own ached.

The mountain rescue team were the first to arrive— trained men who knew what to do once Sir Fergus had assessed the lad's injuries. He and the three men rolled the boy on to the stretcher so that he was lying face down, and then strapped him carefully. They had barely finished this slow and difficult task when the police and the ambulance arrived together.

Rosie stood on one side, and Gyp, at a quiet word from Sir Fergus, stood by her; only when the slow, careful journey back to the road began did she essay to go as well. Sir Fergus had gone with the stretcher, and it was a constable who hailed her.

'If you'll come with me, miss, I'll see you to your car; Sir Fergus has asked us to see you safely home.'

'Oh, has he? I'm absolutely all right to drive, you know.'

'I'm sure you are, miss, but that's what Sir Fergus said—it's only a wee way—I'll drive behind you.'

They were following the stretcher party, and since the progress was slow it was half an hour before they gained the road. Rosie watched them loading the stretcher into the ambulance, a ticklish business which took a few minutes under Sir Fergus's terse directions.

The ambulance doors were shut, the mountain rescue team gathered up their equipment and prepared to leave in their jeep. Rosie walked past the Rolls to her own car, and unlocked the door and got in; there was no sign of Sir Fergus, and the constable had gone to the patrol car to phone and then get in beside his driver, ready to follow her.

The car door opened and Sir Fergus loomed over her. 'Thank you, Rosie. Now go home, have a dram of whisky and a hot bath, and go to bed. That's doctor's orders.'

He closed the door and was gone before she could utter a word, and a moment later his car swept past her to turn and drive back to Fort William, with the ambulance, its lights flashing, hard on its heels.

Rosie turned on the engine and started the drive back to Inverard. Fergus had called her his brave little love, but possibly he said that, or something similar, to any of his patients who showed signs of hysteria. He had kissed her, too—hardly treatment he would give even to the most hysterical of patients. She had been kissed often enough, but never like that. It hadn't meant anything to him. 'Whisky and a hot bath,' she muttered, and clashed the gears going round a corner too fast.

The police car behind edged up a bit. The young lady was driving without due care—not that she could be blamed, it must have been so cold and lonely on the moor waiting for help. A bit of luck that it had been Sir Fergus Cameron who had come by; they had encountered him on various other similar occasions—always calm and resourceful, uncaring of the weather and an expert climber.

It was far into the night when Rosie stopped the car outside her home. The patrol car drew up alongside her, and she got out and went to poke her head through the driver's window.

'Someone is still up. Come on in and have a hot drink and perhaps a sandwich?'

Her father had opened the door, and Hobb came tearing out to meet her. They all went inside, and went through to the kitchen where her mother was pouring boiling water into the teapot. Rosie kissed her and smiled at her father, and introduced the two constables.

'They were kind enough to escort me home,' she explained, and her mother bade them sit down, and fetched more mugs and uncovered a plate of sandwiches.

'Now you've to drive back to Fort William?' she wanted to know. 'It was good of you to come out here with Rosie.' She added carefully in a casual tone, 'You weren't in an accident, love?' She passed round the sandwiches. 'Fergus said you were all right...'

'He phoned? I didn't know.' Rosie bit into a sandwich. 'It was a young man—a boy really, I suppose—walking alone for a dare. He'd got off the West Highland Way and got lost, and then fallen over and hit a rock...'

'Then you came by?' asked her father, turning to the two men.

They explained. 'Not much we could do,' said one of them. 'Sir Fergus was there, and a good thing, too, for the lad had a fractured spine and a broken leg—he'll be at the hospital now, with Sir Fergus sorting him out.

'It's this young lady who saw the boy's torch and went to look for him, and luckily Sir Fergus came driving by after a while. He called us and the mountain rescue team—they've got the right stretchers for rough ground and they know how to handle injuries—and by the time we had all got back to the road the ambulance had arrived. Sir Fergus asked us to escort the young lady home,

'Thanks for the tea and sandwiches. We must be getting back.'

Rosie went with them to the door, and shook hands. 'You know, I don't think I could have driven back on my own. Thank you both very much.'

They assured her that it had been a pleasure, got into their car, and drove off. She went back to the kitchen, and her mother said, 'We're not going to ask you another question—you can tell us tomorrow. Now you're going to have a hot bath, a dram of whisky, and go to your bed.'

'That's what Fergus said,' mumbled Rosie, and burst into tears.

She woke once while it was still dark, her sleepy head full of determination to forget Fergus, never to see him again, never to think of him... She fell asleep again, and when she woke the first thing she thought of was him. Had he been to bed at all? she wondered. And, if so, where? Had he gone back to Edinburgh or was he at home?

Lying there allowing her thoughts to wander wasn't going to do much good; she got up and went down to her breakfast. She had overslept, but her parents were still at the table. Mrs MacFee brought in more coffee and fresh toast and then stood by the door, eager to hear Rosie's account of the accident. She recited it baldly, leaving out as much as she could about Fergus, and when she had finished her mother said,

'Would you like to phone the hospital and ask after the boy? I wonder where he was from?'

'No one from hereabouts,' said Rosie, and went to the phone.

The boy had had emergency surgery, said the voice at the other end of the wire; he had a compound fracture of his left leg and fractured lumber vertebrae. He was paralysed, but there was every hope that it was temporary.

'You were the young lady who found him?' asked the voice.

'Yes,' confirmed Rosie.

'He said to tell you that he was deeply thankful.'

'Oh, please give him my best wishes. He's not local, is he?'

'Glasgow. His parents are on their way here. You're welcome to visit at any time, Miss Macdonald.'

Rosie rang off, and too late wondered how the voice had addressed her by name. It was nice that the boy had a good chance of recovery. She went to tell her mother and, since she felt quite unable to settle to anything, took herself off to the attics.

'There's a bag of odds and ends of wool,' she told her mother. 'It will come in handy once we start knitting; I think it's in the back attic.'

A gloomy little room under the eaves, approached by a narrow passage from the main attic and lighted by a small window overlooking the back of the house, which was why she didn't see the Rolls sailing down the lane to come to a halt before the house door.

'I thought you might come,' said Mrs Macdonald, throwing open the door as Sir Fergus reached the steps. She eyed him in a motherly way. 'You're tired. Were you up all night?'

'Not quite all night.' He smiled down at her. For all his tiredness he looked content and, as usual, beautifully turned out. 'I've come to see Rosie...'

Mrs Macdonald smiled then. 'She's in the back attic—go through the main attic and along a narrow passage—it's the door at the end. It overlooks the kitchen gardens and the river—she won't know... Go up the back stairs, it's quicker.'

Rosie wasn't looking for wool, she was sitting on a very old sofa, its springs sticking out, and eaten by moths. Simpkins was on her lap, and she was staring out of the window, although she wasn't exactly looking at anything; she was, in fact, concentrating upon not thinking about Fergus, and not having much success. The faint squeak of the door opening roused her enough to look over her shoulder to sit, like a small carved statue, gaping at him.

He closed the door behind him, and came into the dim, dusty little room unhurriedly. He lifted Simpkins off her lap with gentle hands, deposited the small creature in an open, battered hat box beside the sofa, and pulled Rosie, just as gently, to her feet.

'Well, now,' he said, 'where had we got to?'

'Got to?' She stared up into his quiet face. 'Where were we going? I didn't know...'

'Of course you didn't, how could you when I had no more time than to kiss you?' He smiled suddenly. 'Which reminds me...'

He wrapped his great arms around her and held her close, and kissed her gently at first and then quite ferociously.

'Well!' exclaimed Rosie, her hair all over the place, struggling to get her breath back. 'Whatever next...?'

A silly question which plainly encouraged him to kiss her again.

At last she asked, 'The girl—the girl you're going to marry. It just won't do—whatever shall we do?'

He held her, if that were possible, a little closer.

'I hope that we shall continue to do what we are doing now, on and off, for the rest of our lives.' He suited the action to the word. 'My darling, you are such a sensible girl, but you have allowed your imagination to run away with you. Did I ever mention this girl by name? Did you ever get so much as a glimpse of her?

And at her muttered, 'I did, I did...' he added,

'Oh—in the car, outside your grandmother's. That was Grizel—a married cousin with four small boys and a doting husband. But did you, in your quieter moments, reflect that a man in love wishes to be with his girl every minute he can spare and, if he can't spare the minutes, talk about her? And did I ever talk about her? And, heaven help me, haven't I spent hours contriving ways and means of seeing you when I should have been doing something else?'

'Oh,' said Rosie, 'do you really mean that?' She caught his eye, and added hastily, 'Yes, you do,' and flung her arms around his neck and kissed him.

'You see,' she explained, 'I didn't like you at first, so I supposed that you didn't like me either, and then when I did like you I thought you were going to be married.'

'I am—to you, just as soon as you can arrange all the tiresome things women want to arrange when they get married.'

'Mother will want us to have a big wedding...'

'Quite right, too; you're far too beautiful to be hidden away. Let her have her wish just as long as she can arrange everything in three weeks.'

'Three weeks? It takes ages...'

'Three weeks or I shall elope with you to Gretna Green!' He kissed the top of her head, which was resting on his shoulder. 'My darling love, not a day longer.'

'Well, if you say so...' She smiled up into his face. 'I'll do my best—I love you very much, Fergus.'

He kissed her for that. 'I love you, my dearest love. Will you marry me?'

'Yes, oh, yes, I will.' She stared up at him, and saw the love in his face. 'We might manage less than three weeks,' she told him.

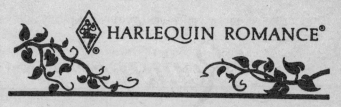

HARLEQUIN ROMANCE®

IF YOU THOUGHT ROMANCE NOVELS WERE ALL THE SAME...LOOK AGAIN!

Our new look begins this September

Harlequin Romance has a fresh new cover that's sure to catch your eye—and our warm, contemporary love stories are sure to touch your heart!

Watch for a sneak preview of our new covers next month!

HARLEQUIN ROMANCE— A lifetime of love

HARLEQUIN
Romance®

**HARLEQUIN ROMANCE
IS IN THE
WEDDING BUSINESS...**

The August title in The Bridal Collection is about...
a wedding consultant!

**THE BEST-MADE PLANS
by Leigh Michaels
Harlequin Romance #3214**

THE BRIDAL COLLECTION

THE BRIDE arranged weddings.
The Groom avoided them.
Their own Wedding was ten years late!

Available in July in
The Bridal Collection:
**BOTH OF THEM
by Rebecca Winters**
Harlequin Romance #3210

Available wherever
Harlequin books are sold.

WED-4

WELCOME TO

The quintessential small town where everyone knows everybody else!

Finally, books that capture the pleasure of tuning in to your favorite TV show!

GREAT READING...GREAT SAVINGS...AND A FABULOUS FREE GIFT!

Each book set in Tyler is a self-contained love story; together, the twelve novels stitch the fabric of the community. The covers honor the old American tradition of quilting; each cover depicts a patch of the large Tyler quilt.

With Tyler you can receive a fabulous gift ABSOLUTELY FREE by collecting proofs-of-purchase found in each Tyler book. And use our special Tyler coupons to save on your next TYLER book purchase.

Join your friends at Tyler for the sixth book, SUNSHINE by Pat Warren, available in August.

When Janice Eber becomes a widow, does her husband's friend David provide more than just friendship?

BIG SUMMER READ

Summer Reading At Its Best

In July, Harlequin and Silhouette bring readers the Big Summer Read Program. Heat up your summer with these four exciting new novels by top Harlequin and Silhouette authors.

SOMEWHERE IN TIME by Barbara Bretton
YESTERDAY COMES TOMORROW by Rebecca Flanders
A DAY IN APRIL by Mary Lynn Baxter
LOVE CHILD by Patricia Coughlin

From time travel to fame and fortune, this program offers something for everyone.

Available at your favorite retail outlet.

BSR

JAYNE ANN KRENTZ

Dreams
Parts One & Two

The warrior died at her feet, his blood running out of the cave entrance and mingling with the waterfall. With his last breath he cursed the woman— told her that her spirit would remain chained in the cave forever until a child was created and born there....

So goes the ancient legend of the Chained Lady and the curse that bound her throughout the ages—until destiny brought Diana Prentice and Colby Savager together under the influence of forces beyond their understanding. Suddenly they were both haunted by dreams that linked past and present, while their waking hours were filled with danger. Only when Colby, Diana's modern-day warrior, learned to love, could those dark forces be vanquished. Only then could Diana set the Chained Lady free....
